NELDA SEES BLUE

A Murder Mystery

By

Helen F. Sheffield

ISBN: 1-4033-1646-5

Library of Congress Control Number: 2002092990

This book is printed on acid free paper.

Printed in the United States of America
Bloomington, IN

1stBooks - rev. 08/01/02

DEDICATION

I dedicate this book to my three children and their spouses: Jim Sheffield and his wife Karen, Deborah Morris and her husband Bill, Carol Lapin and her husband David. They are my most devoted fans.

I also want to thank Marselaine Clarke for her suggestions, and members of Brazos Writers' Fiction Critique Group for their reviews and support.

PROLOGUE

Evening approached. Nelda Simmons and her niece, Sue Grimes, drove into a Shell service station before crossing Lake Pontchartrain into New Orleans. Nelda concentrated on driving her station wagon close to a gas pump while her niece took in all the glitter that a long stretch of lighted bridge could produce from a distance.

When the car came to a stop, Sue jumped out of the car and started the pump. A small sign in the window of a storefront caught her attention as she waited for the tank to fill. PSYCHIC, Constance Marion, IN ATTENDANCE, blinked the sign.

After hanging up the gasoline nozzle, Sue motioned for Nelda to roll down the window. "Look at the shop next door," she exclaimed. "Let's go have our fortunes told."

"I wouldn't waste my money on someone guessing what's in store for me," Nelda said.

"Please, Aunt Nelda, it's only ten bucks, and we are on vacation."

"Oh all right! I surrender. But remember, it's your money."

Nelda studied the neon sign in the large plate glass window, and the faded blue curtains behind it. Reluctantly, she joined Sue by the front door and rang the door bell. Someone peeked out at them from behind the faded, torn curtains. In a few seconds the door opened. There stood a small boy with curly, black hair and eyes as dark as the inky waters of Lake Pontchartrain.

"*Bonsoir*," he said, opening the door wide. "Come in. You here to see Constance?"

"*Oui,*" said Sue trying to show off the little French she knew.

Nelda smiled down at the small boy as they stepped inside. The room smelled of honeysuckle. It brought back childhood memories of gathering flowers in the woods. However, she guessed the fragrance filling this room came from an aerosol can.

The space was divided into two rooms by long strands of multicolored beads that made a swishing sound as the boy left and ran through them. Nelda and Sue sat on an old sofa covered in red velvet and waited for the mystic.

In a few minutes, the beads parted and in walked a slender woman whose straight, black hair hung down to her waist. She had a long thin nose, dark eyes, full lips, and light brown skin with few wrinkles. Her white dress was loose and made of wispy chiffon.

"*Bonsoir,* ladies, I am Constance. My nephew, Gaspar, told me you were here for a reading." She gazed straight ahead.

Nelda thought this was strange behavior until Sue raised her fingers to her eyes and whispered, "She's blind, Aunt Nelda."

"I sense that you have discovered my malady," said Constance spreading her hands out in front of her with palms up. "I cannot see! It happened when I was thirty, a car accident. It was only then that I cultivated my gift of prophesy."

"We're sorry about your accident, but how can you tell our fortunes without your sight? You can't read tea leaves, coffee grounds or even see cards," Sue said in disappointment.

"Madam, just give me ten minutes with each of you. I promise, you will not be disappointed."

"Your idea, Sue. You've got to have a little faith," Nelda said smiling.

Sue struggled out of the low couch and onto her feet. "All right, I'll be first. After you, Constance."

Constance walked over to the beads, pulled them apart and motioned toward a small round table with two chairs. "Please come and sit here."

Sue followed Constance, and the strands of beads closed behind them.

Nelda made herself look at a magazine until Sue's reading was over. Her niece came out smiling.

"Oh, Aunt Nelda, you're going to love Constance. She knew all about me, even guessed the month Walter and I are getting married."

"Really. Guess you got your money's worth," Nelda said skeptically.

"I'll tell you the rest after your turn. I've already paid for you."

Nelda smoothed her long denim shorts and tucked her T-shirt in her waistband before stepping through the beads. Constance was seated, waiting for her with a slight smile on her lips. The smell of honeysuckle was stronger than ever. Nelda looked around and found the source. A huge urn filled with showy flowers stood in the corner.

"I'm a visitor to your state," she said, sitting across from the blind woman.

"It is good that you are here," Constance whispered. "Please allow me to feel some personal item you have had for a long, long time."

Nelda paused, then opening her purse she pulled a small velvet bag from the zippered compartment. Gently, she removed a gold wedding band from the bag and placed it in the psychic's hand.

Constance held the ring in her closed hand, turning it over and over again. She gently rubbed the inside of the ring as though reading the inscription there. Finally she spoke. "I'm sorry for the death of your husband, Madam. I see his name as either James or perhaps Joseph. A big man with strong principles, a man who faced danger many times. You are like him. You've learned many things from your late husband, but you must always be on guard, because someone close to you is ruled by the 3rd zodiacal constellation and will suffer a loss."

Nelda passed her hand in front of Constance's face. The psychic didn't blink. Mumbo jumbo, but how could she know things about Jim? Sue must have told her, thought Nelda.

"You're right," Nelda admitted. "My husband's name was James and I called him Jim. We solved crimes together. Did my niece tell you these things?"

"No," she said in a gentle tone. "You still doubt me, *Cherie*, but I understand. Soon, romance will come into your life, but there will also be suffering."

Nelda shivered and troubled thoughts crowded her mind. The psychic had mentioned danger, romance and suffering. Was a mystery on its way with danger and suffering? Those words didn't conjure up pleasant thoughts for a fun vacation.

"I'd best get back to my niece. It's growing late. Thank you for your insight and advice."

The woman silently gave Nelda's ring back to her. As Nelda stood and turned to leave, the psychic spoke in a low voice. "Beware Madam. *Beware the color blue.*"

CHAPTER ONE

Cajun Reunion

Nelda Simmons sat on the corner of a covered pavilion and listened to Alvin Mouton play his rendition of "Coeur Farouche" (Wild Heart), on an old accordion. She joined a crowd of noisy relatives and friends in keeping time by clapping her hands. Nelda was jubilant because her grandparent's Cajun culture was alive through speech, music, and rich, spicy foods in Louisiana.

In 1755 her Acadian ancestors, French-Canadians, arrived in Louisiana and settled in the rich bayou lands along the Gulf of Mexico. They were expelled from Canada for not swearing allegiance to the British Crown after Great Britain acquired Canada. Through the years, Acadian became known as Cajun.

At the end of the song, Nelda jumped when someone grabbed her shoulder. She turned and embraced her second cousin, Laura Finch, from her hometown of Stearn, Texas. Wonders never cease, thought Nelda. Here I am in New Orleans, several hundred miles from home, and run into a second cousin from my own home town. Laura's mother, Irene, had been Nelda's favorite first cousin. She looked for Laura's teenage daughter, Antara, but couldn't locate her.

"I didn't know you were coming to the Foret shindig," Nelda said pushing her dark brown hair out of her face. Did you come alone?"

"Yes, Antara didn't want to come. She's staying with a friend. I didn't plan this trip until the last minute. Cousin Charley Foret called and said they were having this reunion, so I decided it would be good for me. Anyway, I just had to get away for awhile."

Laura pulled a compact out of her purse, popped it open and ran her fingers nervously through her curly, black hair and patted powder on her nose. Nelda thought Laura looked young for her almost forty years. But what a nervous habit she'd acquired with her fingernail biting. Something was definitely wrong. What? Nelda wondered.

"Will you be going back tomorrow?" Nelda questioned, shouting over the deafening sound of the accordion music, now joined by two loud steel guitars. Her eardrums throbbed.

1

Before Laura answered, she guided Nelda through the crowd of two-steppers dancing to "Le Jour Va Arriver" (The Day Will Come), and into an open area. Her dark eyes filled with tears as she answered. "Yes, I have to be home tomorrow. I'm sorry I haven't seen much of you since I moved back to Stearn, but we really need to talk."

"Let's talk while we're eating," Nelda said.

They both surveyed the food laden tables that lined the courtyard. Nelda grabbed a platter and loaded it with crayfish, crabs, sausage and several rice dishes. Laura picked up a plate too, but spooned the food on reluctantly.

Sitting at a table near the edge of the bayou, Nelda gazed wistfully at the scarlet and white azaleas in full bloom, and the purple flowering wisteria vines that entwined the trunks and limbs of the huge, old oak trees. The perfume from the wisteria was breathtaking. How she wished she could get those plants to grow in her yard, but somehow the soil and moisture were just not right.

Laura pulled her back to the conversation. "Are you still solving cases, Nelda? I've heard about your work with that good looking, young sheriff. What's his name?"

"You're talking about John Moore."

"Before your husband died, wasn't John his deputy?"

"Yes, he's like a son to me. I guess that's why he puts up with me butting into his affairs."

"Well, from what I've heard, you've helped him a lot. You must know everybody in Stearn, don't you?"

"I guess teaching school for thirty years helped me there."

Nelda peeled crayfish tails while they talked and now she dipped them in red sauce and wolfed them down. There were several pitchers of iced tea and beer sitting on the table. She decided to stick to the tea. It wouldn't do for her to have a wreck on the New Orleans freeway. She could see the headlines in the <u>Stearn Gazette</u> now: "LOCAL WIDOW HAS WRECK RETURNING FROM CAJUN BEER BUST."

Her humor faded away as she looked at her cousin. Now was the time to find out Laura's problem. Nelda squeezed lemon in her tea and started working on opening the crabs. "Why don't you tell me what's bothering you?"

Laura sipped on a glass of beer and swallowed a piece of French bread before answering. "My life is a total disaster. You remember how I treated my mother when I was a teenager?"

"Yes, you certainly were a handful. Irene spent plenty of sleepless nights, but you came out of it all right. You're a success."

"Am I? My brother, Ed, doesn't seem to think so. He thinks I was responsible for the fire that killed mother."

"You can't mean that," Nelda said, lifting a fork full of coleslaw. "You were only sixteen."

"I do mean it and the sad part of it is I can't remember what happened before the fire. That part of my life is blank. The only thing I remember is Daddy helping me downstairs just before the fire got out of control. Mother couldn't get out." Tears rolled down her face as she recalled the tragedy.

"I remember Edward was off on his own."

"He was already out of college and working in Dallas. He's been very cold to me since mother's death."

"I'm sorry, Laura. Have you had any contact with him at all?"

"Every chance I get. When he's visiting in town, I make it my business to be at the same social gatherings. We have a speaking relationship, but he's still bitter. You know I'll be forty soon. Then, I'll gain control of the trust Mom and Dad left for me. I know Ed resents that too. He probably thinks I don't deserve it."

"Is that what's bothering you?" Nelda asked, remembering another episode her father had to endure before he died.

"Acting the fool during my teen years wasn't the only mistake I made."

"I remember the birth of Antara without a legitimate father, but you were twenty-four years old then. You're not sorry you had your daughter, are you?"

Before Nelda received an answer, Sue Grimes, Nelda's niece, found them. Nelda gazed fondly at Sue, who was a free spirit without a care in the world. Sue was carrying a tray laden with desserts: pralines, pecan and lemon meringue pies, French cocoa balls, and creamy fudge. They both groaned, but Nelda knew she wouldn't turn down the pralines.

"Laura," said Sue beaming, "imagine having to come all this way to be with you, when we're only a few miles from each other at home." She tossed her long, blonde hair back, set the tray down, and crawled in the seat next to Nelda. Her light blue pantsuit made her eyes even bluer.

"Good to see you too, Sue. You're looking fit as usual. I don't know why you've brought those desserts over here. You must have known I was trying to lose weight."

"Yeah, sure," Sue said eyeballing the skinny brunette. "Where's Antara?"

"She doesn't go anywhere with me anymore—she's almost sixteen. Antara is in love with a car doctor."

"Could be worse," said Nelda, munching on a praline.

"It has been worse, but where are you staying tonight? Laura asked. Maybe we could go out together."

"I've been invited to go to the French Quarter with some of Cousin Charlie's grown kids tonight. Would you and Aunt Nelda like to come? I bet we'll see some wild things," Sue said, grinning.

Nelda wiped her face with a piece of paper towel and answered first. "I can't speak for Laura, but I'm not interested in the nightclub route. When I finish visiting here, I'm going to see the white alligators at the Audubon Zoo, then, if I can eat anymore, I'll have a quiet bite to eat and go to bed. Full day of driving tomorrow. But you, Sue, can sleep on the way back."

"Thanks, Aunt Nelda, that zoo scene seems dull. I'll check that to you. What about you, Laura, want to live it up?"

"Sounds like too much fun for me. I'll opt for the quiet evening with Nelda. See you back in Stearn. By the way, you and Nelda are invited to Antara's sixteenth birthday party next Saturday. We're having a few people over."

"We'll be there," Sue said, as she took the dessert tray over to a group of young people who were swapping stories that ended in gales of laughter.

Nelda wanted desperately to hear more about the reasons for Laura's unhappiness and see if she could help her, but she knew it was impossible now. Several relatives they hadn't seen in years headed their way, yapping it up. "*Mon tende*," laughed Nelda, covering her ear. "We'll finish our talk tonight when we're away from here."

*　*　*

"Well, what did you think of that Louisiana swamp exhibit at the zoo?" Laura asked. Nelda peered out the car window to see if she could make out the name on the street sign. A heavy downpour made it impossible to read the sign.

"It was wonderful! I'm glad the spring shower held off while we were in the swamp. It gave us a feel for how some of the Cajuns lived, but right now I'd like to see a sign with "Crazy Joe's Restaurant" written on it."

"You got it," Laura said pointing to a large sign. "It's straight ahead and the food must be as good as they said it was. Look at all those cars."

"A good omen. I didn't think I would ever be hungry again after what I ate at noon, but I couldn't resist coming here after the relatives bragged about Joe's crayfish etouffe."

Nelda parked the station wagon in the crowded parking lot hoping she'd still have some paint left on her doors when she came back. They sat for a minute and looked at the restaurant through sheets of rain bombarding the windshield. Crazy Joe's cedar board restaurant was built up high on cement piles, with one side adjacent to a large canal. The grounds outside were brightly lit, and large windows made up most of the walls. Suddenly the rain stopped and they ran for the entrance without opening up an umbrella. As they waited in line for a table, Laura fell silent. Worry lines were evident in her face. Nelda hoped she could be of some help to her.

Nelda and Laura sat by a window overlooking the canal. After ordering, they watched with fascination as a group of people sailing down the canal tried to dock their sailboat alongside the restaurant. The sailboat struggled mightily against heavy squalls. Each time they thought the boat had made it close enough for one of the crewmen to jump out on shore to moor the boat, a strong gust of wind drove them

5

back to the middle of the canal. Finally, they made a good landing and everyone on Nelda's side of the restaurant applauded their success.

"I empathized with that crew, Nelda, I'm bucking evil winds, but I doubt that I'll have a safe landing."

"I'm sorry you're estranged from your brother and Antara is giving you a fit. You still have Thomas. I'm sure he's a great comfort to you?"

"I broke off my engagement to Tom. We couldn't see eye to eye on some procedures going on at the fertility clinic he runs in Smitherton, so I'm no longer the technician there."

"Is that why you moved back to Stearn?"

"Yes."

"You want to tell me about that?"

"No, not yet. It's Antara that's breaking my heart."

"Is it more than just being an unruly teenager?"

"Yes! Oh yes. I think she's trying to kill me."

CHAPTER TWO

The Bad Seed

Sue leaned against the back seat of Nelda's car with her eyes closed and relived the fantastic jazz music she'd heard on Bourbon Street. The soul jerking music reverberated in her head, specially that of the sax player, Herbie Dee. He had played as though possessed. Finally, she opened her eyes and stared at Nelda, who drove in silence down the back roads of Texas. She studied Nelda's features and didn't like the frown lines or down turned mouth on her aunt's face. Normally, Nelda's face was smiling and attractive. Sue looked upon Nelda as a surrogate mother, because she's lost her own mother twenty years ago when she was five.

"Okay, out with it," Sue said.

"Out with what?" Nelda asked.

"You never did tell me what the psychic said to you."

"Well, you were so busy basking in your good fortune, I didn't have the opportunity."

"You do now, shoot."

"She said there was danger, romance, suffering, and some kind of zodiacal trouble in my future. Oh yes, and beware the color blue. It's all nonsense."

"Well that takes care of your wardrobe. Everything in it is blue."

Nelda didn't laugh, but looked glum. Sue knew the fortune teller was not the cause of her aunt's depression.

"Okay, which one of our Cajun cousins got under your skin?"

"No, it was nothing like that. Laura has a big problem and I'm worried about her."

Sue smiled. Her problem solving aunt had heard a cousin's tale of woe and wanted to help. "Anyone living with a teenager is in trouble," Sue said. "You remember how rotten I was don't you?"

"Was? Anyway, it's not the same."

"Antara isn't pregnant I hope?"

"No, and I'll tell you what it's about under one condition. You'll not discuss it with anyone." Nelda turned her head and stared into Sue's eyes.

"Cross my heart. Now what's happening to Laura?"

"She told me Antara tried to kill her."

"You're kidding! Sue exclaimed, sitting up straight and frowning in disbelief. "How?"

"Someone cut the lines on Laura's brakes. The only way she could stop her car was to hit a tree. I'm surprised she's still living."

"How did Antara know how to sabotage the brakes?"

"She has a boyfriend who's a mechanic, remember?"

"Why would she want to do away with her mother?"

"It's so complex. Laura still has it in the back of her mind that she may have started the fire that killed her own mother twenty-five years ago."

"You mean Laura can't remember?"

"No! That part of her memory is blanked out."

"Are you telling me that Laura thinks Antara has the bad seed syndrome?"

"She's leaning toward that conclusion, but hopes she's wrong."

"Well, how are you going to help?"

"I don't know," answered Nelda. "I suppose my first step is to get better acquainted with Antara. We're invited to her birthday party next weekend and I'll take it from there."

Nelda fell silent as they covered the last leg of their journey. They were leaving the piney woods and entering the Oak Woods and Prairies ecosystem. Sue could see that smaller trees grew here, and tall pines were replaced by squatty oaks. She remembered the names of the ecosystems from some courses she took in forestry. At that time, Nelda told her that studying fawn and fauna was certainly not in line with the nursing credits she needed. Sue had to agree, but was specially pleased when she could point out some aspect of nature her aunt didn't know. Now she tried it as a diversion tactic to keep Nelda from dwelling on Laura's problems.

"Aren't those bluebonnets and Indian paint brushes on the road sides beautiful, Aunt Nelda?"

"Yes, we picked the perfect time for this trip, cool weather and lots of wildflowers."

"Paintbrushes are semiparasitic. Their roots grow until they reach the roots of certain grasses and then get some of their nourishment from the 'host plant'."

Sue noticed that revelation didn't have the desired effect on Nelda, who sank into another gloomy spell. As much as Nelda loved plants, Sue's wildflower conversation was taking a back seat to Laura's problem.

"You know that's what she said about herself."

"Who? Sue asked with a puzzled look.

"Laura said she was the host or caretaker for everyone around her and was getting weary of it."

"What a strange thing to say. I wonder what she meant by that remark?"

"I suppose the people that she worked for depended on her too much."

Sue gave up trying to distract Nelda. Instead, she asked for some details of the birthday party. "Who's going to be at Antara's party?"

"The noon-time party is for the adults. Laura invited us, her brother Edward, and believe it or not, Thomas, her ex-fiancé, invited himself. It seems he became very fond of Antara while he and Laura were engaged."

"And I suppose the evening party is for Antara's friends?"

"Yes, but I volunteered our services to help Laura with both parties. I didn't think you'd mind."

"Aunt Nelda! You know I always date Walter on Saturday night."

"I know," responded Nelda, "and Walter is invited too. You don't have to stay for the night affair, but if Walter is going to be a member of the family, it's time he met some of the relatives."

Well, why not? Sue thought. It might be interesting to get Walter's opinion of the unbalanced teenager. Oh, Oh! She promised not to tell.

CHAPTER THREE

Old Ghosts

Max Beaux, better known as Crazy Max to his former prison mates, sat in Dennis Toliver's small office with his head hanging down. Most of his face was covered by a gray beard that looked like Spanish moss. His bearded face stood out in contrast to his bald head, usually covered up with a Dallas Cowboy cap which now hung on his knee. Max's coveralls were clean except near the pockets where he wiped his hands.

Dennis sighed as he looked at Max's application, then he spoke. "Been out of Huntsville Prison long?"

"A few months."

"What'd you do?"

"They said it was arson."

"Well, was it?" Dennis asked, giving him a thoughtful look.

"Yes! They put a highway through my daddy's farm and I went crazy. I've paid my debt," said Max without lifting his head.

"I just want you to know I'm willing to give a man a second chance if he wants to go straight."

"I shore do." He lifted his head and looked Dennis in the eye."

"Good, you'll get minimum wages until you prove yourself. My business is lawn care and mowing and taking care of people's plants and other things I can help them with. I'll just give you your assignment every morning and stay with you most of the time until you catch on."

"I appreciate that." Max gazed around the sparsely furnished office. He didn't see anything anybody would want, except maybe the fancy phone and computer. 'Course he knew the warehouse around back was stocked full of lawnmowers, edgers and things that might bring a pretty penny. Right now he intended to keep his nose clean, at least until he got the lay of the land.

"Where are you staying, Max?"

"I got me a little shack by the railroad station. It ain't much, but the rent's cheap."

"You got some way to get around?"

"My sister Charlene's old truck. She loaned it to me until I get on my feet."

"Okay, go over to Producers Co-op on old Main Street and pick up this list of goods. I've already called them. They'll charge it to me, but I want you to check everything off." Dennis reached over and handed Max the list. "Don't worry about your truck upkeep. I'll help you on that."

"Thank you, that's mighty generous of you."

"Come on back here as soon as you can; we've got work to do."

Max shuffled out of the office and climbed into his sister's old Chevy. Well, maybe things were looking up. He had a job, transportation, a place to stay, and the yearning for that old thrill was just a memory.

He whistled "Tom Dooley" as the old truck smoked its way over to the Co-op. When he got there, he studied the list to make sure he knew what was on it: fertilizer, mulch, fabric gazebo, six folding chairs, forty watt bug killer and gopher poison. "What's all this junk for?" He mumbled to himself as his grimy fingernail outlined poison.

* * *

Max was welcomed back to the office by Dennis, who was filling a large wall calendar with work assignments. He acted pleased with Max's first job effort, because Max indicated everything on the Co-op shopping list was in the truck.

They walked outside and Dennis examined the purchases. "Glad you could find everything. Now let's go start that job I promised to do. The place is located off Black Prairie Road and belongs to Nelda Simmons' cousin. Do you remember Nelda? She's a retired school teacher and has lived here forever."

"Can't say that I do," he said gruffly. "My folks had a farm ten miles out. Didn't know too many city folks." Max tried to forget the past. He didn't want all those bad memories to come rushing back. Maybe he oughta leave town and find some other place to live. Charlene talked him into coming back, but it just weren't right.

11

They loaded all the supplies in Dennis' shiny new truck. It had been years since Max rode in a new truck. He slid into the front seat and breathed in the smell of newness as they moved out. Some day soon he'd have one like this; he just knew it.

Max enjoyed looking at all the gadgets on the dashboard, and he could tell she was burning gasoline as clean as a whistle. There weren't no blue smoke snaking along behind them. It was the best ride he'd had since getting out of the pen.

Pretty soon they turned off Black Prairie Road into Oakwood Estates. Max could see mail boxes on posts by the side of the road, but sometimes it was hard to see the homes they serviced. Most of the homes were sitting so far back in the woods you couldn't see them from the road. He marveled at the way the countryside had developed since he was a boy. These woods were the ones where he and his brother Elmo used to hunt rabbits in when he was a kid.

Finally, Dennis slowed down and turned into a long, graveled driveway. The place looked oddly familiar to Max. He could see a big, two story log house with stone chimneys and wrap around porch. Grandfather rocking chairs and a wooden swing on the porch gave the place a homey look. Then he spotted a mailbox standing in a clump of weeds with the name of its owner painted on the side, "L. Finch."

The sight of the surname caused tremors to start in Max's hands. He broke out in a cold sweat and finally hid his hands in his pockets to stop the shaking. All the old ghosts were coming back to haunt him.

By the time they drove up to the log house and parked, Max had his feelings under control. He marveled at the picturesque look of the place. The back had a glassed-in porch leading out to a terraced deck.

He looked over at Dennis and said, "It looks just like a picture, don't it?'

"Well I guess your eyes slid over the wooden fence that's down in the front, and the paint flaking off the house logs."

"Rekon they did."

"Ms. Finch is having a birthday party for her daughter. We're going to get the yard all cleaned up today, and tomorrow we'll be coming back to help them decorate."

Max stared at the log house for any sign of life. He just didn't know if he could face those people who lived there are not. Being stuck in the Big House for a number of years makes you want to hide from folks. You just don't trust the outside world.

Dennis jolted him back to the reason he was there. "Why don't you put all these supplies in that big storage shed over there? Be sure to put the gopher poison way up on a top shelf."

The old shed held a number of yard tools, including a wheelbarrow. Max rolled it out to the pickup truck, and Dennis helped him fill it with supplies from the Co-op. While Dennis went off to gas up the lawnmowers, Max started putting things away in the shed. He gingerly lifted the gopher poison to the top shelf and discovered there was poison already there in an old rusty can. The can's label was brown and flaky, but the skull and cross bones stood out in bold warning.

"Well I declare," whispered Max as he pulled the can off the shelf and unscrewed the top. Looking inside the can, he found it half full of small white crystals. He replaced the lid and shoved the can to the back of the shelf. A back door slammed; he turned to see a girl watching him from the redwood deck. Fear made him tremble. Old ghosts were beginning to gather.

CHAPTER FOUR

Malcontent

The alarm clock made a shrill noise at 5:00 a.m. on Saturday morning. It forced the couple in the dark bedroom to wake up. Edward Finch pounded the off button of the clock and sat up in bed. He stretched, flexed his well-built muscles and groaned. His bed mate stared at the back of his dark curly head and laughed.

"My, didn't we wake up in a good mood," crooned Angelique Ware. Is Old Grouch doing something he doesn't want to do today?" She threw one leg across him.

Edward, having never denied himself sexual gratification, growled back and bit her playfully on the leg. She wrapped her arms around him and licked at his ear. In the next few minutes, squeals of feminine laughter faded away to soft little moans. Finally, Angelique rolled on her back, flipped on the bedside lamp, and watched as Edward made his finale by brushing his lips on her skin from her navel to her mouth. Before she could embrace him again, he made for the shower.

* * *

Angelique pouted while Edward stood before the dresser mirror knotting his tie.

"You don't even like your sister. Why are you going to your niece's birthday party and leaving me all alone for the weekend? I might do something naughty," she said while twisting the sheet into a rope.

"I don't like it anymore than you do, but where else am I going to get a loan? I'll help Laura celebrate her brat's birthday if that's what it takes. Maybe you and I can take a cruise to the Bahamas if this works out."

"Do you really believe Laura started the fire that killed your mother?"

Edward reached in the closet, pulled out a light blue summer sport coat and slipped it on before answering. "Yes, she was that kind of rotten kid. Mom and Dad gave her everything, but it was never enough. I had to work my way through school, but she didn't lift a finger."

"Did she say she'd give you a loan? It seems you're taking a lot for granted."

"Why shouldn't she? I'm her brother and she's receiving twice as much as I did when I turned forty."

"Why?" Angelique asked, frowning at a chipped fingernail.

"Her estate holdings have doubled in value since dad died. I've got to go. I'll call you."

Edward kissed her lightly on the lips before swinging his garment bag over his shoulder. He left the room without a backward look. Angelique heard the front door slam and his Jag start with a roar. Only then did she pick up the phone.

*   *   *

Edward slipped a CD in the player as he cruised down I- 45 toward Stearn. His selection was "Fly" by Gary Semonian. For a while, he leaned back on the leather seat and enjoyed the music and feel of the car on the road. Then an anguished question swirled in his mind. What would he have to give up if Laura wouldn't give him a loan? All would be lost: country club membership, car, house, and beautiful, auburn-headed Angilique, who would never stay with a loser. Bankruptcy was sure to follow. Life would be a bitch!

Trying to push his fears aside, he tried to remember who Laura said would be at Antara's birthday party. The first guest Laura had mentioned was their older cousin, Nelda Simmons. Several years had passed since he'd seen Nelda, but he remembered her passion for getting people in or out of trouble, depending on their guilt or innocence. Almost everyone seemed to like her, but he was uncomfortable around her. It was as though she could read his thoughts. He laughed ruefully and vowed to watch his act around her.

Now, Sue, Nelda's neice would certainly be a pleasure to see. He was sure she was now in her mid-twenties, blonde and beautiful. Yes indeed, he thought smiling; she could easily become his kissing cousin.

Sue's escort would be her employer, Walter Goodman, who was a medical doctor. They'd probably need a doctor if they had to eat Laura's cooking. Edward hoped Walter wasn't too boring. Oh well, he'd only be with him for a few hours.

The only other adult invited was Thomas Compton. Edward couldn't help wondering why Thomas and Laurie split. He seemed a nice enough guy. How many men will she find who would want a forty year old woman with a teenager? Maybe Thomas would try harder to make up, if he knew the amount of money Laura was going to inherit.

As he neared his destination, his thoughts turned to the plea he'd make to Laura for a loan. Why was it he felt like the biblical Cain? He knew why! By birthright the estate should be his. He shuddered inwardly knowing someone he despised held his future.

CHAPTER FIVE

Scorned Lover

There was an eerie silence in the laboratory as Thomas Compton peered suspiciously around the room, searching every nook and corner with his eyes. All labs involved with human reproduction seemed to be targets for kooks who couldn't mind their own business. He was continually on the lookout for those trouble makers. When he was satisfied there were no intruders: he removed his glasses, washed his hands, and bent his long, thin body to look at a slide under a microscope. Usually, the sterile quietness of the room soothed him, but today it created unrest. If only Laura were still around to make me laugh, he thought. Thomas moved the slide around on the stage of the instrument and then pushed it away with disgust. Laura wouldn't leave his thoughts. In his imagination, he saw her smiling face framed by thick, black hair, but the image faded away. "How in the hell did she think I was going to change what I'm doing? My hands are tied and she knows it," he grumbled, shaking his head. The door opened quietly behind him.

"Good morning," said a thin, young Chinese man dressed in a white lab coat.

Thomas glanced around and saw his assistant, Chy Yang, holding a tray of petri dishes. Chy set the tray down and carefully locked the entry door.

"I'll be gone today," Thomas said.

"Laura."

"Yes."

Chy regarded Thomas solemnly. "Is she still leaving?"

"As far as I know," Thomas said as he walked over to a sink and once again washed his hands, before taking his white jacket off and dropping it in a receptacle with a fitted top.

"But you'll persuade her to come back?"

"Do my best."

"Good," Chy said, "We've worked together for eighteen years. She needs to be here."

17

When Thomas left, he locked the door behind him and made sure the "No Admittance" sign was in place.

*　*　*

While making the thirty-minute drive to Stearn, Thomas had a lot to think about. The most important goal in his life was the success of his fertility clinic. For years he had worked to obtain loans, make good investments and seek grants to open such a facility, and now it was paying. Nothing would stand in the way of his success, even Laura. She knew what the prosperity of the clinic meant to him. Once more he would beg her to come back, but if that didn't work, he'd go on without her. It would be difficult finding someone to fill the void left by her absence. Who could he get to replace her?

CHAPTER SIX

The Awakening

The sun's rays shining through the half-closed blind made the water sparkle in the bottle of Canadian Aqua on Antara's bedside table. She made little smacking noises with her lips while trying to open her eyelids. Suddenly the peal of the telephone woke her. Brushing her thick, unnaturally red hair out of her face, she searched the bedside table for the noisemaker, but only succeeded in knocking the spring water to the floor. Kicking off the sheet, she slid on her stomach to the edge of the mattress and located the telephone under a dirty T-shirt. Finally, she held the receiver to her ear and said hello.

"Antara, Derek here. You sound down under."

She giggled, flopped over on her back, and stared at a life-sized picture of the teen movie star, Mike Damus, riding on a surfboard. It was thumbtacked to the ceiling.

"Hey Big Bird," she said, "know what today is?"

"Hurley Davidson's birthday? The day Henry Ford invented the Model-T?"

"No, dipstick. It's my birthday."

"Cool, I knew that. Thought you were talking about something important here."

"You big grease monkey! Get over here. We need to set up for tonight; fifty of us are gonna party."

"I'll be over, chick, but what about those noon-day stiffs?"

"Just a bunch of Mom's friends and relatives. Like, who cares? Forget 'em!"

"See you in an hour, Birthday Girl."

Antara hung up the phone, reached for a pillow and hugged it to her chest. Sixteen candles. Ha! Did it mean more freedom? No, not from Mom, the Iron Duchess. There was no escape or was there?"

Suddenly there was a gentle knock on the door. Antara called out loudly, "Come on in, Mom."

Laura opened the door and stood in the doorway with a big smile on her face. She was already dressed for the day in yellow pants and matching shirt that contrasted the beauty of her dark hair and olive complexion.

"Happy Birthday, sweetheart. Better get cracking. We've got lots of things to do before our guests arrive."

"Sure, Mom. I'll be down in a little bit."

Laura opened her mouth as if to speak, but then shut her eyes and mouth quickly. When she opened her eyes, she waved good-bye and quietly closed the door.

Antara knew why her mother wouldn't step into the room. The bedroom floor was completely covered up with Antara's clothes. Her clothes' closet and dresser drawers stood open and empty. The smell of candle wax mingled with the odor of smelly tennis shoes and leftover pizza. She knew her room was a total disaster, and a source of many arguments between the two of them. Who knows what the day might bring? Maybe she'd do something special for her mother.

CHAPTER SEVEN

First Guest

As Nelda drove up in Laura's driveway, she stopped and looked at the old, two-story log house with apprehension. It was such a dreary place, the ideal home to dredge up unpleasant memories if there were any in your past. Three huge oak trees spread their branches in front of the house providing complete shade for the railed porch. Large ferns hung from the porch roof trailing their long fronds to the lichen-spotted floor, while grandfather rocking chairs moved back and forth as though already occupied.

Nelda wondered why Laura came back to her parents' old homestead. She should be living close to people, so she could mingle and have contact with the outside world. No wonder she was depressed.

She drove further down the long driveway to the back of the house. To her astonishment, she saw Dennis Toliver whom she hadn't seen in a long time. Dennis used to mow and trim her lawn, but last year he started taking on landscaping jobs and had raised his fees. Nelda could no longer afford his services. She and Dennis shared a common interest in collecting old comic books. She missed their weekly visits.

Dennis opened Nelda's car door. "Hello, Nelda. It's good to see you."

"Hi Dennis. I guess I'm just in time to help you get ready for this affair, huh?"

"We could stand some help," Dennis said smiling down at Nelda with clear blue eyes and unruly blonde hair bleached white by the sun. Every time Nelda saw Dennis, she marveled at his resemblance to the comic book character, Archie.

Suddenly, Max shuffled out of the old storage shed dragging two folding chairs behind him. He glanced furtively their way before picking the chairs up and walking toward the gazebo.

"Who's that you have with you, Dennis?"

"My new man, Max Beaux; do you know him?"

21

"No, but the last name rings a bell. I believe they were farmers, lived right outside of town. They operated a vegetable stand in the summer."

"He did say his folks farmed."

The back door slammed. Nelda and Dennis looked toward the house to see Laura walking toward them. As the two women embraced, Nelda could sense the anxiety of her younger cousin. Her body was tense.

"I'm glad you came early, Nelda. Maybe we can visit before the others get here."

"I hope so. I'm also anxious to see the birthday girl."

"Antara is upstairs. Go talk to her while I show Dennis where to set up the volleyball net."

"I'll be back to help," Nelda said, as she turned and followed an old brick path back to the house.

Once inside the house, Nelda found herself transported back in time. Laura had furnished the downstairs with beautiful antiques. One large room with exposed beams served as both living and dining room. The fireplace, made of limestone from the Texas Hill Country, occupied one end of the room and supported a mantle made from a thick cedar plank. A walnut china cabinet, filled with cut glass and sterling silver pieces, occupied one wall of the dining room. The large dining room table and eight high-back chairs looked right at home with the pine log walls forming a backdrop. In front of the fireplace was an elegant Sheraton sofa in pale rose velvet, several Queen Anne's chairs and a hexagonal cocktail table of rosewood. Lamp tables and expensive lamps completed the furnishings. Nelda's eyes widened. Where had Laura gotten the money to furnish the house with all these expensive pieces? Had her job been that lucrative?

As Nelda climbed the pine staircase, she realized why Laura had moved back home instead of buying in town. The many windows in the house let you see the woods without going outside. It was wonderful, but the restoration of the house and grounds would require a lot of hard work. Dennis and Max had their work cut out for them.

Nelda didn't have any problem finding Antara's room. The rock music was going full blast. How did the poor child keep from hurting her eardrums? After knocking on the bedroom door several times, with no results, Nelda pushed open the door and stuck her head in the room. She could see Antara sitting in front of her dresser mirror brushing her hair. Except for the blue lipstick, white eye shadow and bright red hair, Antara bore a striking resemblance to her mother. Nelda cringed at the sight of wall to wall dirty clothes, books, soda cans and other cast-off items on Antara's bedroom floor. Before she could back out of the room, Antara spotted her, turned off the CD player and flashed her a grin.

"Nelda, come on in. Mother said you and Sue were coming today. Don't mind the mess on the floor. It seems there is never enough time to clean it up. But what difference does it make anyway? You just have to do it all over again."

Nelda wanted to speak out about the condition of the bedroom, but knew this wasn't the time. "Happy sixteen," she said. "You look just like your Mom, except for the red, white and blue."

"Cool isn't it? My teachers have the same reaction to my dyed red hair and blue lips as Mom does, nag, nag nag."

"I guess the condition of your room is really a statement too?"

"You bet," said Antara warming up to the conversation.

"Would it surprise you to know that your mom had the same fixation about her room when she was growing up?"

"You're kidding!"

"No, she wanted to do her own thing, just like you."

"Then, she should know how I feel."

"She loves you, Antara."

"That's what she says, but I have no freedom. I'll have some soon."

"What do you mean?"

Antara wore a determined look and avoided Nelda's eyes. "There's relief on the way, now let's go downstairs. Let the party begin." Antara wiggled her hips in her tight jeans and tousled her red hair with one hand as she escorted Nelda down the hall.

Nelda shook her head. She could only speculate as to what the Birthday Girl had on her mind.

CHAPTER EIGHT

Birthday Toast

All the adult guests had arrived. Nelda surveyed the group with a great deal of curiosity. Thomas and Edward were busy hanging colorful paper lanterns on a wire line strung between two large oak trees. They made periodic trips to the old shed where the lanterns were stored. Nelda noticed they weren't doing much talking, but they both looked up every time the back door slammed. Were they waiting for Laura to appear?

"Hey, Aunt Nelda," shouted Sue, "come sit with Walter and me."

Walter and Sue were dressed in blue jeans and T-shirts. Sue's shirt had a "Don't mess with me" sign on it. Nelda had to laugh, because Sue was the opposite of being aggressive. Walter's shirt, reflecting the prim and proper doctor that he was, had nothing on it. They were a handsome couple, no doubt about it. Nelda hoped something good (like a marriage) would come from this relationship.

She ambled over toward them for two reasons, one, to chat with her favorite niece, and two, to get a good vantage point for watching the other guests.

"Did you see Dennis here, Aunt Nelda? He's got some horrible looking man working with him."

"Sue, don't be so judgmental!" Walter said. "Maybe, the man just fell on hard times."

"He must have fallen hard," Sue said, "judging from the way he looks and acts."

Nelda shook her head without commenting. Sue was right; there was something about Max that wasn't quite normal. The man acted like a fugitive, always glancing around to see if anyone was watching him. How did Dennis end up hiring him?

Laura opened the back door and headed for the storage shed. She carried a small notebook and pencil in her hand. The door of the building was open and Nelda could see her moving chairs around as though she were counting them. Abruptly, Edward quit hanging lanterns and hurried over to talk to Laura. Everyone looked startled when he raised his voice. He shouted, "It's not fair!" Then he rushed out, banging the door behind him. He approached the back door of the house in a huff and disappeared inside.

Hesitating, Nelda wondered if she should go to Laura and see if she could help solve the disagreement. Before she had time to act, Thomas walked briskly over to the shed and had a whispered conversation with Laura. She couldn't see the expression on Laura's face, but eventually Laura turned her back to Thomas and he left to finish his lantern-hanging chore alone.

Derek Stalling, Antara's current flame, had parked his Harley-Davidson motorcycle in the shade. As he placed a cover over it, he eyeballed Edward's Jag enviously. The gold earrings he wore in both ears glinted under his long, greasy, slicked-back hair. Nelda just knew that in the wintertime he wore a black leather jacket, like Fonzie in the old "Happy Days" TV series.

Laura came out of the shed and waved to everyone and smiled. "Antara, would you please come and help me bring lemonade out to our guests. The food will arrive soon. I have hired the best caterer in town. When Dennis and Max get the tables up and cleaned off, I'll call 'Suzanne's Deli' to bring the food."

Everyone stood around chatting amicably while Dennis and Max cleaned the tables off, arranged them end to end, and spread pink tablecloths over them. Antara's birthday gifts were down on one end of the, now long table. Nelda hoped her gift of a silver ankle bracelet was not too old fashioned for the cool teenager.

Finally, Antara, her mother, and Edward emerged with trays filled with glasses, pink lemonade, bowls of extra sugar, ice cubes and spoons. Antara filled the glasses and invited everyone, including Dennis and Max, to come and get a drink.

A phone rang. Laura placed her drink on the edge of the table, and ran to answer the portable phone under the gazebo. "Foods on its way," she called, coming back to pick up her lemonade. She made a face when she sipped her drink and added more sugar. After a thorough stirring she lifted her glass.

"Let's drink to Antara's birthday and the wonderful life she has ahead of her," her mother said.

25

Nelda noticed that Thomas raised his glass to Laura and their eyes met. He smiled. Could it be his flame was still burning for Laura?

"Here, here," came the chorus, as they all toasted Antara with lemonade. It was a warm day and it didn't take them long to down their drinks and ask for more. Antara busied herself opening the gifts, while they waited for the food. The first gift she opened was a beautiful, yellow shirt from Walter and Sue. Before Antara opened her second gift, Walter's beeper went off and he had to excuse himself to make a phone call.

Nelda watched Sue make a face; she knew what that pager meant. Walter had an emergency call from the hospital and wouldn't be able to stay. Sure enough, Walter made his apologies to Antara and Laura. Sue waved good-bye to him as he backed out of the drive. Such is the life of a doctor, thought Nelda. If Sue married Walter, this situation could be their weekend norm.

Nelda looked up to find Laura doubled over in pain. "Laura, what's wrong," she asked?

"I'm not feeling well; just help me back to the house, Nelda. You stay, Antara, and finish opening your gifts. I'll be all right in a few minutes."

If Walter hadn't just driven off, he'd know what to do, Nelda thought, as Laura leaned heavily on her and moaned softly. Fortunately, the master bedroom was on the first floor and Nelda quickly got Laura on the bed and helped her stretch her legs. She unbuckled Laura's shoes, while wondering what else she could do. Could be something she ate, Nelda thought.

"Have you eaten anything today, Laura?"

"No, soup last night." A series of convulsions raked her body as her arms jerked out in front of her.

Nelda knew Laura was in big trouble. She ran out to the backyard to ask Sue to care for her while she called 911. She'd almost forgotten Sue was a nurse and could do more for her than she could. Antara and Sue ran to the bedroom together.

The hospital was thirty miles away. Would Laura die en route to the hospital? She dialed frantically, and was told they would send an ambulance immediately. Nelda rushed back into the bedroom.

"I think it's poison, Sue, is there anything we can do?"

26

"Someone poisoned her?" Sue asked, opening her eyes wide.

"I don't know, but there's a good possibility." Nelda twisted the ring on her finger in frustration.

"In that case, we can't make her throw up, because we don't know what it is. It could do damage coming back up. Milk, yes, milk would be good for her to drink. Antara, hurry, get your mother a glass of milk."

Antara took off for the kitchen, while Sue stood deep in thought. Finally she spoke, "Oh yes, Aunt Nelda, there is a universal antidote. It consists of strong tea, milk of magnesia and burned toast. But I've forgotten the proportions."

"By the time we found all the ingredients, the ambulance will be here. Let's just try to get her to drink the milk," Nelda replied.

When Antara returned with the milk, they tried unsuccessfully to get the milk down Laura. She twisted and turned involuntarily. Matters were taking a turn for the worse.

The party had broken up when Antara rushed to her mother's side, and the food vendor, having recently arrived, was sent away. The guests huddled together in the living room, looking miserable. Nelda observed their reactions as she waited for some sign of the ambulance: Derek nervously hit his fist in his open hand; Thomas excused himself to use the bathroom, and Edward paced up and down with his head lowered. Standing on the front porch, Dennis and Max talked as they stared down the road. Max, his beard looking bushier than ever, was leaning on the handle of a yard broom.

As Nelda reentered the bedroom, she noticed Laura's skin had turned blue. Not enough oxygen, Nelda guessed. *Nelda sees blue.* Could this be one of the omens predicted by the fortune teller? Laura mumbled something as Nelda knelt by her side. She put her ear close to Laura's mouth and thought she heard her say, "Take care of Jimmy Nigh." What could it mean? Was this the name of someone responsible for her condition?

Antara became hysterical and screamed, "Mother, Mother, I love you. Please don't die!" Finally, Sue led her out of the room as Laura had another convulsion.

It was twenty minutes before the ambulance arrived. Nelda watched as they quickly loaded Laura into the ambulance and accepted Sue's offer to ride with them. Nelda promised Laura she'd drive Antara to the hospital, but was not sure her ailing cousin was aware of her presence.

Before they left for the hospital, Nelda hurried out to the tables covered with pink tablecloths and looked for the glass that held Laura's lemonade. It wasn't there! She counted all the glasses and one was missing. Who, she wondered, was the demented person responsible for posioning Laura.

CHAPTER NINE

Nelda's Dilemma

Following the ambulance that carried Laura to the hospital was an agonizing trip for Nelda, because of Antara's emotional state. Antara was beside herself with grief and guilt. Nelda knew it was because of her previous battles with her mother and now her mother's illness. It proved to be more than the sixteen year old could handle.

"Why did this happen?" Antara said between sobs. "You know I love her, Nelda, and I'm sorry I treated her so...bad! Please, please, God, don't let mother die. I promise to be a better daughter." Antara buried her face in her hands.

Nelda felt compassion for the girl and wished she wasn't driving so she could hold and comfort her. She vowed to find who was responsible for Laura's illness. Because of Laura's bluish skin color and convulsions, Nelda was braced for the worst possible scenario, murder.

She used her right hand to pat Antara on the shoulder. "Don't give up, Antara, we're almost at the hospital, and then we'll see what the doctors can do for her. Be brave for her sake."

Once at the hospital, Nelda drove up to the emergency entrance. She let Antara out, before looking for a place to park. Parking spaces for visitors were hard to come by, but Nelda was lucky enough to find someone backing out of a spot. She quickly filled it.

To Nelda's surprise, Sue was waiting for her in front of the emergency entrance with tears streaming down her face. "What's happening, Sue? Were they able to help Laura?"

"I'm afraid not," she said, while dabbing at her eyes with a tissue. They think it's strychnine. Her body has already absorbed it. The convulsions won't kill her, but the poison shuts down the respiratory system. She seems to have had a massive dose of the poison. Somebody really wanted her dead."

"Where's Antara, Sue? I let her out before I parked the car." Nelda started twisting the ring on her finger.

29

"I don't know; I didn't see her, but Antara will not be allowed to see her mother. Laura's convulsions are really terrible." Sue held the door open for Nelda.

When they entered the hospital, they found Antara leaning against the hall wall, right outside the emergency room. She was in a terrible state with red, swollen eyes and hands that trembled as she talked. New tears flooded her face when she saw them.

"They can't stop the convulsions, Nelda. Mother is going to die!" She hugged herself and looked down at the polished linoleum blocks.

Nelda took Antara's arm and guided her to a chair. "Let's give them a chance. Sit over here with us until the doctor gives his report.

Nelda felt guilty and frustrated. She had witnessed her cousin drinking the deadly poison, but didn't know it. What could she have done to stop the poisoning? Laura's words spoken to her in New Orleans came back to haunt her, "It's Antara that's breaking my heart. I think she's trying to kill me".

*　　*　　*

The next day dawned bright and clear, but Laura was dead. She died during the wee hours of the morning. Now, here they all were in Laura's log house: Antara, Derek, Max, Dennis, Sue, Walter, Thomas and Edward. They gathered together at the request of the sheriff's office. Emotions seemed to be under control, even Antara's, as they waited gloomily for the sheriff to appear.

Nelda sat on the Shearton sofa with her arm around Antara's shoulder, while speaking to Sue. "At least we'll have a friend in Sheriff John Moore."

Sue smiled, "Well he'd better be. Uncle Jim taught him everything he knows."

"Who is this Uncle Jim?" Thomas asked. He was standing at the window watching a couple of playful squirrels run up a large pin oak tree.

"Nelda's late husband; he was sheriff forever and John was his deputy." Sue answered while rubbing the tired muscles in her shoulders.

Derek slouched in from the kitchen followed by Edward with a tray of coffee. Nelda wondered if she could handle another cup of coffee. She decided that if she bled right now her blood would be dark brown, but she appreciated the men's efforts.

"I must say," Edward said putting the tray down on the coffee table. "That unkempt creature that Dennis hired is acting awfully strange. He won't even stay in the house, but asked Dennis to sit in the backyard with him."

That's all right with me," Sue said snuggling closer to Walter, "Max gives me the willies."

Walter frowned as he spoke, "How long do you think the sheriff will keep us, Nelda? I've got a lot of work to do."

"I don't know," she said.

They were all exhausted. Antara had gone to sleep with her head in Nelda's lap. Nelda had tried earlier to get her to stay in bed, but she wouldn't hear of it.

Walking away from the window, Thomas said, "A pickup truck just turned into the drive."

Nelda slipped a cushion under Antara's head, walked to the window and looked out. "That's not John's truck, unless he got a new one." She opened the door then stepped out on the porch.

A short, stout, moon faced man with a ruddy complexion climbed out of the truck. He wore a khaki uniform, cowboy hat and polished boots that gleamed in the morning light. There was a notebook tucked under his arm and he carried an expensive camera. At the edge of the porch, he stopped and held out a thick hand.

"I'm Joe Coates, the acting sheriff. I hope you all got my message and can help me out. Doctor Goodman briefed me on your situation here, so maybe I can speed things up." He stared at Nelda with eyes as blue as an Aspen sky.

Nelda sees blue. Oh please thought Nelda, this man couldn't cause the romance forecast by the psychic. She shook his hand and was surprised to find it hard and callused. "We're all here, but we were expecting John Moore." Nelda couldn't keep the disappointment out of her voice. "What's happened to him?"

"Nothing. The state sent him for some schooling, instead I'm in charge 'till he gets back." He took off his hat. "You a friend of John's?"

Joe was no spring chicken, Nelda noticed; his hair was mostly gray. "Yes, I'm Nelda Simmons. John was my late husband's deputy." Nelda twisted on her ruby ring, a birthday gift from Sue.

"I've heard of you, Ms. Simmons. Seems like you've kept busy helping John solve several crimes." His eyes narrowed and his lips made two thin lines, as if to convey it wouldn't happen to him.

"I think I was a little help. Come on in; we're all gathered in the living room except for the two in the backyard. I'll get them for you."

Nelda held the door open, but Joe didn't move. He studied the hat in his hand for a moment or two before speaking, "Now, Ms. Simmons, I don't want to get crossways with you, but I figure I better tell you now. The Sheriff's Department will be working alone on this case. We don't want the public interfering. They could get hurt. You understand my position don't you?" His beefy hands rolled the edge of his hat.

"Yes, as long as you do your job right in finding my cousin's murderer, you won't hear from me." She gave the ring on her finger one final twist before walking back in the house.

Joe walked in after Nelda, introduced himself, then placed his hat on the mantle.

After opening his notebook, he scanned the room until his eyes came to rest on Derek. "What's your name, son?"

Derek brushed his long, black hair back from his gold earrings, before answering with a smirk. "Derek Stallings, Sir."

"How about asking those two in the backyard to come in here? I need to talk to them."

"Sure thing." Derek slammed out the back door waking up Antara. She sat up with a startled expression on her face, gazed around the room then bowed her head.

When Derek returned with Dennis and Max, they walked over to the dining room table and sat down. Max never looked directly at the sheriff, but pulled a soiled, red handkerchief out of his pocket and rubbed his eyes. Joe acknowledged their entrance with a nod as everyone looked at him expectantly.

32

"As you know, I'm here to investigate the death of Ms. Laura Finch. The doctor who attended her in the hospital believes she died of strychnine poisoning. We'll know for sure by tomorrow. I understand that some of you are from out of town. That's why I asked for the meeting today. I'll want a statement from you before you leave town.

"Now here's what I want to do, with your permission, of course. I'd like to take a picture of each of you. Then, when you give your statement, I'll put the picture with it. This will help us have a clearer picture of what happened yesterday."

"Well, I protest!" Dennis said, standing. "There's no use in treating us like a bunch of criminals. Wait until you find out if it's murder." Indignantly, he looked at Nelda for support.

"The sheriff stared at Dennis. "Tolliver is your name, isn't it? You're the man that looks after the grounds at Central Bank, next to the sheriff's office."

"That's right, I'm Dennis Toliver and this is my helper, Max Beaux." He put his hand on Max's shoulder. We were just out here helping Ms. Finch get ready for her daughter's birthday party. Neither of us know anything about her private life."

"I'm still going to need a statement from you. Does anyone else object to me taking pictures?" Joe asked, picking up his camera.

There were no more objections as the sheriff took down the name and address of each person before snapping a picture. Even though Nelda was mad enough to step on the sheriff's shiny boots for telling her to butt out of his case, she thought a photo, along with the suspect's statement, was a good idea. Sheriff Coats was new to the county. He didn't know all the local folks as John did.

"I want to interview all of you in my office this afternoon about thirty minutes apart, so if you'll come over as I call your name, I'll give you a time. That way, you out-of- town people can go on home when I finish with you."

"Just one other thing," he pointed to Nelda. "Ms. Simmons, could I see you in the kitchen for a minute? Excuse me folks, I'll be right back." He retrieved his hat from the mantel, then followed her to the kitchen.

Nelda wondered what in the dickens the sheriff wanted with her, it certainly wasn't her help. He'd already made that clear. Joe walked the length of the kitchen, while Nelda stopped at the work island in the middle of the room. "What can I do for you, Sheriff?"

"Does Ms. Finch's daughter, Antara, have anyone to stay with her? She can't live in the house by herself." He rubbed his brow as if searching for a solution.

"Well of course she can't," Nelda said. She wondered if Antara had thought of the situation she was in now. "I know she'll want to remain in school here, so she can't go back with her uncle. She has a great aunt who lives here. Don't you worry about Antara, Sheriff, I'll see that she's taken care of." She looked up to find him scanning the counter tops and cabinets.

"One other thing, I understand from talking to Dr. Goodman that the poison might have been in her lemonade. Have the glasses been washed?" He looked directly at her.

"No, but Laura's glass is missing. I gathered the rest of them after slipping on rubber gloves." Nelda opened the pantry to show him where she had stored the unwashed glasses and pitcher with lemonade still in it.

"Now isn't that interesting," he said. Sweat was forming on his upper lip and his brown eyes showed annoyance. "How did you know hers was missing?"

"I ran back to collect the glasses and lemonade before we started for the hospital. I remembered she put her glass down in the left corner of the long table." All at once Nelda felt incredibly tired.

"To your knowledge, did any of the *guests* have a motive for killing your cousin?"

Nelda felt tremendous relief for the way the question was worded. She wouldn't have to tell this stranger the story of "The Bad Seed". "No," she answered truthfully, "I have no idea how her death would benefit any of the guests."

CHAPTER TEN

Blood Will Tell

Nelda's appointment with the sheriff was at four. Sheriff Coates had placed her time after the others, for what reason she couldn't fathom. Well, she thought, he'd just better not give me an ultimatum to butt out of his business again. Nelda had a burning desire to solve this mystery involving her family.

Standing in the high-ceilinged bedroom of her old ancestral home, Nelda had the impulse to wear her new, blue dress for her interview with the sheriff. *This one blue thing she didn't have to beware of.* Although he had hurt her feelings by not allowing her to be a part of the investigation, she liked his honesty. She liked the way he stood up to her, and there was something very attractive about his looks, like a weathered tree, made rugged by outdoor elements and time.

After she dressed, Nelda checked her messages and found one from Edward. "Nelda, sorry I can't visit with you today. Right after I talk to the sheriff, I have to head back to Dallas. Robert Lavish, is executor of Laura's and our parents' estates. I tried to reach him, but he was out. Could you go by and talk to him about Antara? She'll need some funds while staying with Aunt Mary. Call you later."

So generous of Edward to volunteer her time to take care of his niece's needs. Not that he didn't care for Antara, but Edward always came first. His needs were more pressing and it had always been so. Nelda remembered him as a small child who wouldn't share his toys. Nothing had changed, except his toys were bigger and more expensive.

She picked up the phone to call Robert, a prosperous lawyer and friend of her late husband, Jim. They had gone all the way through college together. After Jim died, she saw less and less of Robert and his wife, Susan. Nelda knew this was one of the problems of being a widow. You just don't fit in with couples anymore. Robert's secretary answered the phone on the second ring. A few seconds later Nelda heard the baritone voice of her old friend. She could just see him sitting at his huge mahogany desk: a beefy, baldheaded guy with his feet propped up, tie loosened, and a cup of hot coffee in his hand.

"Nelda, terrible news about your cousin. Poor little Antara. How is she taking all this?"

"Not well."

"I can imagine. I tried to get in touch with Edward. I want to attend the funeral. Where is Antara?"

"Antara will be living with her great aunt, Mary Finch. There's not going to be much of a funeral, because Laura wanted to be cremated and have a simple graveside service."

"I heard it was murder."

"Yes."

"Who would want to harm her?"

"I couldn't even venture a guess; it's a real puzzle. It was Antara's 16th birthday party. What possible motive could someone have?" She was hoping that Robert would volunteer some information about the wills without her asking. "Edward wanted me to call and ask you to release funds from the estate of his parents for Antara. Mary is on a limited income and will need money to care for Antara."

"Of course. I guess Edward told you that I'm handling both his parents' and Laura's estates. Antara will not be poor. I'll get some money to her Aunt Mary right away."

"Who receives the money from the parents' estate? Will Edward receive another portion?" She held her breath until he could answer.

"Yes. Edward will share the rest of his parents' estate with Antara even though he got his half when he was forty. He had fun spending it, from what I understand. This document will be public record in a few weeks, but until then please don't repeat what I'm saying. I'm telling you this, so you won't worry about Antara."

Nelda frowned and bit her lip. Edward had a motive for killing Laura and so did Antara. No! Antara couldn't kill her own mother. It just couldn't be true. Her mind kept going back to the scene in Crazy JO's Restaurant. Laura's words came back like an echo, "It's Antara who's breaking my heart. I think she's trying to kill me."

"Is Edward, Antara's guardian?" Nelda asked.

"No. She doesn't have a legal guardian, but I suppose I'll play that part until she's eighteen."

Nelda shifted her attention to the kitchen clock. She'd best hurry or she'd be late for her appointment with the sheriff.

"Thanks, Robert, for taking care of the funds. Gotta run, give Susan my love."

"Will do. I'll take care of Antara."

Grabbing her list of things to do, she charged out the door and paused at the edge of her long covered porch. It always thrilled Nelda to see her blooming bougainvilleas, their long vines laden with beautiful red flowers. They were planted in two large baskets hanging from the ceiling at the end of the porch. Nelda had a way with plants, and had solved more than one mystery while toiling in her flower beds.

* * *

The sheriff's office looked just like it had when Nelda was there last summer helping John gather information about the murder of Dr. Coldsby. Big oak trees lined the parking lot and squirrels played among their branches. The office was just a simple red brick building with room enough for a small lobby and several offices.

Nelda didn't see any cars she could recognize. In fact there were very few in the parking lot. She pulled her jade green Ford wagon under a tree and rolled the windows down an inch all around. The weatherman had promised the temperature would be in the nineties.

* * *

Joe Coates looked out the window of his office and saw Nelda getting out of her car. Nelda, he conceded, was nosey but smart and he couldn't complain about her looks or straight talk. She didn't act one bit like his late wife, Eva, who was as sweet as those chocolates she had craved, and she certainly hadn't wanted to know anything about his work. Maybe, that's why he got off to a bad start with Nelda. He just wasn't used to a female solving crimes. John Moore could probably use the help, being a young sheriff and all, but an old mossback like himself didn't want to invite the grief of being obliged to a female. Wouldn't hurt him to freshen up, he decided.

He stared at himself in the little mirror over the sink, and had to admit his hair looked a lot like gray tumbleweed. As he forced a comb through it, he grudgingly admitted he needed to visit the barbershop. It was strange for him to have an interest in his looks. After Eva died, he thought he would never care whether a woman looked at him twice again. However, he might be able to get more information out of Nelda, if he didn't put up such a tough front. She could help without being directly involved in the investigation. Joe tried to smooth out the wrinkles in his shirt by retucking his shirttail in his trousers, then returned to his office. After straightening the papers on his desk, he sat down and waited for his last witness.

*   *   *

Nelda decided as she entered the sheriff's office that she'd be reserved in her conversation with Joe, but at the same time try to glean some information she could use to solve the crime. It was just a shame that they couldn't work together. She knew she could help him if given the chance.

In the outer office was the same secretary she'd known for twenty years. "Vera, how are you? Grandkids doing okay?"

"Hi, Nelda. I'm just fine and those kids of mine are working me overtime with baby-sitting."

Nelda was childless, and could only imagine what it was like to baby-sit. She'd taught high school for thirty years, but little kids seemed to require a lot more time and patience.

"How's the new sheriff treating you?" Nelda inquired.

"He's sure different from John. Sort of keeps everything to himself. But he seems to have a handle on everything."

"When is John coming back to his office?"

"Not sure. He's attending that sheriff's school in Dallas for several months. I've seen him only once since he left."

Vera didn't have time to say more. Joe opened his office door and invited Nelda inside. Nelda was surprised when he invited her to sit down, and actually pulled a chair out for her. She guessed manners were still alive with some of the older men.

"Thank you for coming in, Nelda. Would you care for some coffee?"

"Yes, I'd enjoy that. Black's fine." Unlike John's coffee, that used to smell as if something was burning, Joe's coffee smelled fresh.

He walked over to the coffee pot and started talking as he poured the coffee.

"I just wanted to go over the events that occurred at the birthday party. Would you tell me exactly what happened from the time you arrived until the time Laura got sick?"

Nelda admired the clean desk, and waited for him to sit down before she started talking. She didn't have to look over a messy stack of papers to see Joe sitting on the other side of the desk. A far cry from the way John used to run things. But still, she missed him and wished he was back.

After she took a sip of the coffee he handed her, Nelda started with her dissertation of what happened the day Laura drank the poison. "I arrived before lunch time to help Laura get ready for the adult party that was planned for noon, also the teen party planned for that evening. Dennis Toliver and his helper, Max Beaux, were already there in the backyard getting things in place. When Laura came out the back door, I went in to see Antara. She was dressing upstairs."

"Nelda, do you mind if I tape this?" Joe pointed to a recorder sitting on the end of the desk. "My note taking is so bad that sometimes I can't read my own handwriting." He laughed, showing her scribbling in his notebook.

Nelda doubted that his hand writing was that bad. He just wanted to hear, maybe more than once, what she had to say. He'd probably listen for uncertainty or anxiety in her voice. Still, why should she mind? She didn't intend to lie to him.

"Sure, why not. You can put that with the Polaroid picture you took of me. It will probably be worth a lot of money some day." Nelda grinned, enjoying herself.

Joe punched the record button. "You were saying that Max and Dennis were already there and you had gone upstairs to talk with Antara."

"That's right. After Antara and I visited, we walked out to the backyard. In a little while all the guests arrived within minutes of each other. Walter Goodman, the local doctor, with my niece Sue Grimes; Edward Finch, Laura's brother from Dallas; Thomas Compton, Laura's ex-fiancé, and Derek something or other, Antara's boyfriend."

"I understand that some people were helping get things out of the shed and set up for the teen party that was supposed to take place later." Joe rolled a yellow pencil on the top of his desk as he talked.

"Yes, Dennis and Max visited the shed out in back, but so did Edward and Thomas. Sue and Walter, to my knowledge, didn't do anything but sit under a tree. I didn't see Derek in the shed either."

Joe turned off the recorder. "Nelda, I think the poison that killed your cousin Laura came from the storage shed."

This news took Nelda by surprise. She thought that whoever put the strychnine in the lemonade had brought it along that day. If it was stored in the shed, maybe it was not premeditated murder, but on the spur of the moment. Edward argued with Laura in that shed and Thomas had a hushed conversation with her, too. Should she tell that to the sheriff?

"What was that poison doing in the shed, Joe?"

"Actually, there were two boxes of gopher poison in there. One was an old box and the other was recently purchased by Dennis. Both boxes had Max's fingerprints on them." Joe got up and took a folder out of the files. He shoved a photograph of the two boxes of poison over to Nelda.

"I'm sure Dennis bought this new box to poison gophers. Max, as his helper, probably stored it in the shed and also handled the other box."

"Nelda, I'm giving you this information for a reason." He turned the recorder back on. "Do you know anything about the conversations Edward and Thomas had with Laura in the shed?"

"No, I heard Edward arguing with Laura, but couldn't make out what he said. After he left the shed, Thomas had a whispered

40

conversation with her. I have no idea what they discussed. Didn't they give you that information when you talked to them?"

Joe walked to the window and looked outside. Nelda thought it was probably where he wanted to be. It was a beautiful day, specially made for an outdoors man. The feet in those well-worn boots must be itching to be on real ground.

"Yes, Nelda, I got some answers from everybody. I'll tell you this too. Old Max made quite a reputation for himself a few years back, burned down several homes. It seems these homes belonged to people responsible for building the road that took his daddy's farm. Laura's parents' home was one that was gutted by a fire."

"What! You think Old Max was responsible for setting fire to the Finch's home twenty-four years ago, and now he's out to get her?"

"He's my prime suspect. Max had the motive and the means."

"Joe, anyone could have slipped the poison in her glass. Laura set her glass of lemonade down on one end of the table while she used the phone. All of us passed by her glass to receive lemonade and then for refills."

"Not everyone had a motive, especially a grudge that's simmered for over twenty years." He turned the tape recorder off and rewound it.

Nelda didn't say a word. She didn't know anything about Max. However, she thought Joe was really stretching to accuse Max of murder. Donald, on the other hand, could now live the life he had grown accustomed to because of Laura's death. And what about Antara? She wanted to be free of her mother.

CHAPTER ELEVEN

Fly Away

Red dust, boiling up from Jones' road, covered Nelda's Ford station wagon. Nelda and Sue followed behind a line of cars headed toward Peace and Harmony Cemetery.

"I tell you, Aunt Nelda, it's too hot for a memorial service." Sue pulled on the collar of her gray gingham dress and angled the side air vent so the cool air could blow on her face.

Nelda nodded. "My poor car. I just had it washed yesterday. Why don't they pave this road? I feel sorry for the people that live along here."

"I feel sorry for them for more than one reason. Can you imagine living in one of those shacks?"

"Sue, I'm sure it's not by choice they're living there. We don't know what their circumstances are. However, lack of education might have something to do with it."

"Yes, I know how you feel about everyone having an education."

Nelda grinned. Sue had heard that sermon before. Nelda was one of the county's biggest supporter of higher education.

Sue sighed. "Are we almost there?"

"Yes, and I bet there is not one tree in the whole cemetery we can use for shade."

"Why did Mary choose the hottest part of the day to have the service?"

"That was Edward's doing. God only knows why."

After a few more miles of dust and heat they arrived. There were no roads leading into the cemetery. Everyone parked on the side of the highway. They walked in through a rusty iron gate decorated with wire angels.

Nelda was wrong about no trees. Nevertheless she reached under the seat for her umbrella and opened it up when she got out of the car. There was a big oak tree near the block of graves reserved for the Finches. She and Sue made a bee line for its shade. Nelda closed her small umbrella and waited for the others to gather near the graves of Laura's mother and father.

Antara, holding Derek's hand, walked slowly behind her Aunt Mary, who was carrying a white urn. Edward, looking a little rumpled, walked alongside Robert Lavish.

Robert held a white handkerchief to his forehead, but he was already drenched with perspiration. Thomas entered the gates with an attractive blonde woman whose dark glasses covered most of her face. The woman fanned herself with a plastic folder while talking to Thomas in a whisper. They all stopped near the oak tree as though waiting for someone to start the service. Finally, a small yellow VW drove up and stopped at the gate. Out jumped a man Nelda recognized as a retired Baptist minister and friend of Mary's. He hurried over to Mary and Antara, said a few words to them, and then the service began.

"We are gathered here to pay our last respects to Laura Finch..."

The minister ended with a prayer and turned the service over to the blonde woman who had arrived with Thomas. The minister introduced her as Yvonne Sands, a roommate of Laura's from her college days. Yvonne spoke in a low, pleasing tone mixed with tearful emotion.

"I was so saddened by the news of Laura's death. She was closer to me than my sisters. We talked every week on the phone, and shared all our joys and disappointments. I've lost my very best friend. I shall always remember the great times we had together..."

Now, it dawned on Nelda who she was. Little Yvonne Sands was not so little anymore. Her hair had also changed from brown to blonde. While growing up, she was Stearn's most talented actress in the little theater. Yvonne had shocked everyone by running away with the town's bad boy after graduating from high school. Fortunately, it took only a year for her to come to her senses. That's when she entered the University of Texas at Austin, and excelled in voice. Nelda wondered where she lived now.

The memorial ended with Antara scattering the ashes of her mother over the graves of Laura's parents, while Yvonne sang an old gospel song, *I'll Fly Away*. "Some bright morn when this life is o'er, I'll fly away. To a land on God's celestial shore, I'll fly away. I'll fly away oh Lordy, I'll fly away. When I die hallelujah, by and by, I'll fly away."

Nelda and Sue brushed tears away. An afternoon breeze came out of nowhere to help Antara scatter the ashes. Laura's earthly remains filled the air around them. Nelda thought it a most appropriate ending to a very sad drama.

The ceremony was all over in less than thirty minutes. Nelda looked around her. All the suspects were here except Old Max. She wondered why the sheriff didn't come to observe. He could have watched the reactions of those attending the service. Not that he could solve the crime that way, but you never know when a clue might turn up. She guessed that Mary hadn't informed him the memorial was taking place.

"Sue, I'm going over to talk to Yvonne. You want to come with me?'

"No, Aunt Nelda. I'll say good-bye to Antara and Mary for you."

Nelda caught up with Yvonne going out the gate. "Yvonne, I hardly recognized you with your blonde hair. That was a beautiful testimonial you gave for Laura, and I know she would have thought, "*I'll Fly Away*," was just right."

"Thank you, Nelda, it's so good to see you." Yvonne hugged Nelda. "I wish I had time to visit, but I've a plane to catch."

"Where are you living now?" Nelda asked.

"In Houston. I'm choir director of the Holy Baptist Church there."

"Do you have a business card? I do want to visit with you when you have the time."

Yvonne opened her bag, dug through it quickly, and produced a business card. Nelda put it in her pocket and watched Yvonne rush off to Thomas' sensible Volvo. He was waiting for her. Nelda waved good-bye as the dust filled the air behind them.

Someone put a hand on Nelda's shoulder and she jumped. She turned and discovered the sheriff drenched in sweat. He looked absolutely miserable.

"Sorry I startled you, Nelda. I just wanted to say hello."

"I didn't think you were here. How could I have missed you?" Nelda asked.

"My truck is on the other side of the cemetery. I was standing behind that big gray monument." He pointed to a statue in back of where Nelda and Sue had been.

"They were all here, Sheriff. All the suspects were here except Max."

"You're wrong, Nelda. They were all here." He pointed to two men walking on the other side of the cemetery. She could make out the figures of Dennis and Max as they hurried to get out of the heat.

It made Nelda ill to think that one of the mourners was probably the murderer. He or she had come to see the final chapter in Laura's life.

As if reading her thoughts, the sheriff said quietly, "The killer will pay, I promise you that."

Nelda bowed her head and hurried toward her car. Sue was waiting there for her. After they buckled up, Nelda pulled out into the road. Thank goodness they wouldn't be eating anyone else's dust on the way back.

"The service was nice, Aunt Nelda, but awfully sad. Laura's college room-mate said some wonderful things about Laura. I wonder why Thomas didn't say something?"

"Maybe he wasn't asked to. He seemed detached about the whole affair, but he seems fond of Antara."

They were quiet on the way back. Nelda knew it was time to take time out and write down everything she knew about the case. She would also find a way to interview all the suspects.

"Aunt Nelda, you just passed up my apartment," Sue said in an exasperated voice.

"I'm sorry, Sue. My mind was on other things."

"I know. When you get on a case, that's all you can think about." She hesitated and then said, "But I love you anyway."

Nelda patted Sue on the shoulder before backing up and letting her out. "Good-bye, Sue, and thanks for going with me."

Tomorrow, Nelda thought as she headed home, she'd make something happen. She just knew it.

45

CHAPTER TWELVE

Into the Past

The early morning sun found Nelda in her flower garden pulling weeds. She scolded herself for allowing weeds and grass to grow among her American Beauty roses. Her wide brimmed hat cast a broad shadow on the ground as she knelt to spade and pull out those prolific invaders. Thoughts of homes burning, strychnine poisoning, and wayward teenagers made her yank the Johnson grass out with a vengeance. Around noon, she ran out of energy and decided she'd done enough weeding for one day.

After shedding her work hat, smock and shoes, she padded to the kitchen to fix lunch. Nelda heard the water rumbling through the old pipes as she filled the tea kettle to make iced tea. The water made her think of Laura's poisoned lemonade. If Laura's killer dumped strychnine crystals in the lemonade, how did they dissolve so quickly? She knew, from her science background, that the crystals weren't very soluble in water and especially ice water. There were so many unanswered questions. Still mulling over the problem, she ate her tuna fish sandwich and drank tea. Her thoughts were interrupted by the telephone. It was Sue.

"Aunt Nelda, I have the afternoon off. Let's have lunch and visit Antara when she gets in from school."

"Too late for lunch, Sue, but I'll pick you up at three to visit her. Be sure to call Mary and tell her we're coming."

Nelda looked down at her grubby feet and knew she'd just have time to take a shower and visit Dennis before meeting Sue. Dennis, an ex-student of Nelda's, would certainly tell her everything he knew about his employee, Max. It was a mystery to her why Dennis had hired him. Although thinking back, he had always wanted to help those in trouble. Max fit that category. Nelda dialed Dennis' number and waited impatiently for him to pick up the receiver. He answered on the fifth ring.

"Dennis' Lawn and Landscaping," was the business-like greeting.

Nelda smiled, visualizing him in his cluttered little office, surrounded by sacks of fertilizer and garden tools. There was such a wholesome air about him. Besides that, he had the courage to defy the old unwritten law that says a man shouldn't marry an older woman. His beautiful wife, Marcie, was several years older than he was. They were good friends of Nelda's.

"Dennis, this is Nelda. I'd like to talk with you about Laura's death. Could we meet downtown and have a cold drink together?"

"Why sure, Ms. Simmons. I've got some free time about two. How about City Cafe?"

Nelda said she'd be there at two. Before hanging up, she was positive someone was listening on the line. There was a faint click before Dennis said goodbye. But then, phones acted strange sometimes, so she dismissed it from her mind.

Early afternoon traffic was heavy. Nelda had a hard time finding a parking spot in the small area designated for the City Cafe. On her way to the entrance, she waved to several townspeople driving down Main Street. She was third generation resident of Stearn and knew most of the people in town.

After entering the old cafe, she paused inside to allow her senses to adjust to the gloom and smells of the old building. Odors from fried food and cigarette smoke hung in the air. The interior hadn't changed much from the fifties. It sported a low ceiling with fans that turned lazily over a dozen or so small tables covered with red checkered oil cloths. No one seated you here. If you saw an empty table, you grabbed it.

"Over here," called Dennis from a table in the corner.

Making her way over to his table, Nelda stopped to say hello to her neighbor, Martha Hillman, who took care of Nelda's plants when she took a trip. In the back of her mind, Nelda could see several trips coming on. After a hurried conversation with her about the weather, she finally arrived at Dennis' table.

Dennis got up and pulled out a chair. "Good to see you, Ms. Simmons. I guess you've had your interview with the new sheriff." After seating her and sitting down, he added, "I don't especially like him."

Helen Sheffield

"Well, why not?" Nelda asked, as she moved the catsup and hot pepper bottles to the side of the table. She couldn't concentrate on her conversation when barriers were between her and the speaker; but now her fingers were sticky. As Nelda scrubbed her hand with a napkin, Dennis tried to get the attention of the waitress.

"How about me ordering us something to eat or drink before we talk?" He asked.

"Thanks, I'll have a Diet Coke in a can." Nelda didn't think the plastic drinking glasses would pass the Good Housekeeping Seal of approval.

Dennis laughed at Nelda's order in a can. He called the waitress over and asked for a can of Diet Cola and iced tea.

"Now tell me, Dennis, why on earth did you hire old Max? He doesn't look or act trustworthy and the sheriff said he was in prison for arson."

He shook his head and rubbed the back of his neck in frustration. "See, that's why that sheriff and I can't get along. He's not willing to give the poor old fellow a chance? Max made a mistake, paid his debt and I'm just trying to help him out by giving him a job."

Their drinks arrived and Nelda wiped the top of the can with her napkin before taking a sip of the tepid drink. She decided next time she'd choose the meeting place. The fans weren't even moving fast enough to push the limited amount of cool air around.

"I'm sorry, Dennis, but I can't stand this place another minute. This is one time I wouldn't mind getting rid of a landmark. I rate this cafe a two on a scale of ten. Let's just sit out in my car with the A/C going."

Dennis drained his glass of iced tea and followed Nelda out to her car after paying for the drinks. Nelda's car gave them a blast of hot air when they opened the doors; but in a few minutes, with the A/C going, they were quite comfortable. She intended to make the conversation as short as possible. Nelda didn't want to heat up the engine of her car.

"Did Max tell you whose houses he burned and why he did it?"

"Sure, Ms. Simmons. He said they were the people responsible for his daddy's farm being confiscated so they could build a road. The county highway cut right through their property and his daddy

48

died of grief over it. Wasn't a thing his family could do about the sale." Dennis' eyes became teary.

"Well, I know that's a shame, but that's called 'eminent domain' and it's perfectly legal. The state has the power to condemn and appropriate private property for public use. They had to pay them for it."

"Yes, but not enough to buy another place. Max just went berserk when it happened."

"Dennis," said Nelda, staring directly into his eyes, "Laura's mother, who was my favorite first cousin, died in flames set by someone during the same period."

"No, Ms. Simmons," Dennis shook his head emphatically, "Max did not torch the inside of that house. He never confessed to that crime, claims he didn't do it."

Nelda was silent for a minute wondering what the truth might be. Had Laura set the fire that killed her mother? Research was the key to the truth about those house fires.

"We're going to heat up your motor, just sitting here," cautioned Dennis.

"You're right. I've got to let you get back to work. Thanks for meeting with me."

Dennis stepped out the door, but Nelda remembered about the poison. "Just a couple of questions about the poison. Did Max know there were two boxes of poison in the shed? Did he handle them both?"

"Yes, the sheriff said his fingerprints were the only ones on the boxes of poison. Max told me he just picked up the old box, looked at the little white crystals inside and then put it on a higher shelf. There was no reason for him killing Ms. Finch, was there?"

"Not that I know of," Nelda conceded. "Dennis, just watch Max." She rolled the window up after asking him to say hello to Marcie.

*   *   *

School was out for the day. Nelda and Sue were on their way to Mary Finch's patio home. Stopping behind a big, yellow school bus,

Nelda watched the kids jump off the bus and run in front of the stopped traffic without looking right or left.

"Look at that, Sue. They're trusting little souls aren't they?"

"They sure are. Little do they know I might be driving," she said and laughed.

Sue looked radiant in a red, cotton dress that matched her shoes. Nelda supposed being in love enhanced her beauty. It gave her a special chemistry that even affected her frame of mind. She was enjoying her niece's happiness, but not this stop and go.

She looked over at Sue and groaned. "I wished we'd started a little earlier. Now we're stuck behind this school bus."

"Can't be helped, Aunt Nelda. How do you suppose Antara has adjusted to living with Mary?"

"She couldn't possibly be adjusted yet and especially under such sad circumstances. But my question is, how will Mary adjust to Antara?" Nelda remembered the condition of Antara's room when she visited her on her birthday; she knew Mary could very well be in shock about now.

"Aunt Nelda, I hate to bring this up, but it's bugging me. On the way back from the family reunion, you told me Laura thought Antara was trying to kill her. What do you think about that now?"

"Oh Sue, I've thought of that so many times. It's all so complicated. Remember, I told you Laura had a fixation about the 'bad seed' syndrome."

"That's crazy, aunt Nelda."

"I know," she said stopping in back of the bus for the third time.

When the bus turned on another street, Nelda breathed a sigh of relief. She finally drove into Mary's modern subdivision and stopped in front of her patio home. Nelda shuddered at the sight, no large trees anywhere. After Mary's husband died, she sold her big house and bought this smaller one with a postage stamp yard. There were two bedrooms and two baths, so theoretically she and Antara had enough privacy from one another. Nelda was eager to see how it was going, and how Mary was coping with Antara's boyfriend, the motorcycle man.

"Does Antara have a car?" Sue asked.

"No, she doesn't have her driver's license yet. Her Aunt Mary confided in me that she was happy about that. She thought she'd worry less about Antara if she didn't have wheels."

Nelda wondered at that reasoning when Derek Stalling rode up on his motorcycle, with Antara perched behind him. He sported a body T-shirt, greasy blue jeans and fancy, dark glasses held on with a black elastic band. Thank goodness both had sense enough to wear helmets.

Sue and Nelda got out of the car and walked toward Antara as Derek backed his motorcycle out of the drive. He waved to them as he roared down the street.

"Hello, Antara," said Nelda as she embraced the teenager. "I see you've got your own chauffeur."

Antara gave them a sad little smile as she pulled her helmet off. "Derek would have hung around, but he's late for work."

She had deep circles under her eyes and her wild, red hair was brushed back and secured with a black, velvet ribbon. Already, Nelda could see the influence of Mary.

"Well how are things going?" Sue asked.

"Okay, I guess. I miss mom so much and wanted to stay in my room, but Aunt Mary convinced me I needed to get out of the house. Derek took me to school this afternoon to pick up my grades."

Mary opened the door and smiled broadly. "Nelda and Sue, how nice of you to visit us. Come on in."

She led them into a large room that served as a living and dining area. The room held antiques crowned by fine linen scarves with lace borders. Figurines sat in the middle of crocheted doilies. A cluster of ancestral portraits in gorgeous old frames hung in the dining room. Nelda knew she had to come back for a closer look at the antiques and maybe get a history lesson on how Mary acquired the old pieces.

"Nelda, would you'll like to sit on my covered patio? It borders the golf course and there's always a breeze blowing out there."

"Sure, Mary. I love all your antiques and hope you invite me back for a closer look."

"You're always welcome."

They all sat down around a large cedar table on the patio. After a few minutes, Mary excused herself to go for refreshments and Sue offered to go with her. Nelda took advantage of being alone with Antara.

"Antara, your mother told me at the family reunion that the brakes on her car had been tampered with and it caused her to have a wreck. Do you know anything about that?"

"I remember when it happened. But I don't really know anything about cars. I suppose someone could have done something to the brakes to make them fail."

"Where did she take it to have it fixed?"

"Farr's garage. Their tow truck came out to pick it up."

"Did you mention this to the sheriff?"

"No, I just didn't think about it being important."

Sue and Mary returned from the kitchen with a tray of fresh cookies and drinks. Nelda decided not to question Antara any further about Laura's accident in the car.

"This is so nice out here," Nelda said. "How lucky you are to have such a wonderful view."

"I'm so lucky to have Antara keeping me company." Mary gazed fondly at the young girl and continued talking. "Antara picked up her grades at school today. Her school counselor tells me she's a fine student. How did you do this time, dear?"

Antara handed her Aunt Mary the report. Nelda was happy with the way Antara was treating Mary. Maybe something good would come out of this terrible situation.

Mary beamed as she handed the card to Sue and Nelda. "All A's and B's," she said.

Antara looked at Nelda, burst into tears and ran into the house. Nelda saw an A in auto mechanics on Antara's report card. She shook her head wondering why Antara lied about her knowledge of cars.

CHAPTER THIRTEEN

The Run-in

On the way to Farr's garage, Sue bombarded Nelda with questions. "Aunt Nelda, why did Antara run out of the room crying?"

"Because she told me she didn't know anything about cars."

"I see. It's the "A" in auto mechanics that got her into trouble."

"Yes," Nelda said softly. "How could she make such a good grade in that course and not know anything about a car's brakes?"

"Do you believe she cut the brake hose on her mother's car?" She raised her eyebrows in dismay.

"No! No, I don't. She was lying for another reason." Nelda slammed on her brakes as a red VW whipped into the small space in front of her. She sounded her horn and grumbled under her breath. "Can't even leave a space in between you and the next car, because those fools fill it up."

"Why would she lie?" Sue asked, oblivious to their near collision.

"I don't know, but I intend to find out."

Farr's Garage loomed ahead. A big tin barn surrounded by junk cars, and car parts lying around everywhere. Regardless of his surroundings, Nelda knew there couldn't be a better mechanic then Johnnie Farr.

As Nelda pulled up in the yard, Johnnie sauntered out of his barn. He was a gaunt man with long, gray hair, and a surprisingly young unlined face. His overalls were covered with grease as were his hands.

Nelda got out of the car smiling, but Sue didn't budge. She took a long look at the clutter, before opening up a new *Time* magazine.

"Hello, Johnnie." Nelda said, keeping her distance.

"Howdy, Ms. Simmons. Don't tell me your new Ford is already giving you trouble?"

"No, it's running fine. I just wanted to ask you about my cousin's car. Her name is Laura Finch."

"Hey, that's that murdered woman." Frowning, he removed a red rag from his back pocket and scrubbed on his hands before he continued speaking. "You know, I called the sheriff when I saw her picture in the paper. I just knew the man who cut her brake hose finally got her."

Nelda looked grim. "Why do you think it was a man?"

"Well, Ms. Simmons, I shore wouldn't think a woman would know how to use a balde." He squinted at her through strands of hair that reminded Nelda of vertical blinds.

"What did the sheriff say?"

"Not much, just wanted to know what I thought about it."

Johnny pulled himself up on the hood of an old car and sat down. Nelda was amazed that he didn't let out a yell after sitting on the hood of the sizzling car. He just hooked his thumbs under his coverall straps, and acted like he was the key witness in the murder case. Undoubtedly, the sheriff had really built up Johnny's self esteem.

"How did you answer him?"

"I said it was a sharp knife that done it. Then after we talked, he wrapped what was left of the hose in newspaper and left."

"Thanks, Johnny, I appreciate you telling me about Laura's car."

"No problem, Mam. I just want to help find the killer."

Nelda opened the car door and got in. As she buckled up, Johnny slid off the old car and walked over. She lowered the window.

"One other thing, Ms. Simmons," he said with hands on hips. "The sheriff wants me to call him if anybody comes nosing around about the car."

That figures, thought Nelda. Joe Coates, the disagreeable sheriff, was going to be an obstacle at every turn.

* * *

After Nelda dropped Sue off at her apartment, she went home and found two messages on her phone recorder. One was from Antara, asking Nelda to meet with her at 8:00 that night at the public library, and the other was from Joe Coates saying he would drop by at 5:30. Nelda looked at her watch. Just time to water the flowers in the front yard before he arrived. She needed some distraction before she faced this disagreeable man. Oh, if John was just back in his old job. Nelda hated confronting the new sheriff.

To her dismay the red petunias planted in the large pots on her porch were wilting. She had forgotten to water them with all the commotion going on. Nelda especially wanted these to be healthy because the hummingbirds loved them. She hurriedly filled the sprinkling can and had just finished watering when Joe Coates arrived.

"Hello, Nelda," Joe said as he slammed the car door.

"Hello, yourself. What brings you out so late?"

"I hear you've been pretty busy." Joe stopped talking as though he was waiting for a confession.

Nelda put the can down on a bench at one end of the porch. "Not busy enough," she answered, "I've sadly neglected my flowers."

"Could we talk in the shade?" Joe asked. He ran his fingers inside his collar. His khaki shirt looked stiff and uncomfortably hot.

"Why don't we sit on the back porch," Nelda said leading the way around the house to a long wooden porch. "This is my favorite retreat in the early morning light for coffee and in the evening for something cold to drink. Could I offer you anything?"

"No, thank you," said Joe sinking down in a grandfather rocking chair. "This is not a social visit, Nelda. I'm concerned about you interfering in my murder investigation."

She didn't answer right away, just pushed her hair back, then brushed the dirt off her skirt with a small brush she found on the steps.

"I wasn't aware that I was interfering with your sheriff's duties."

"You were at Farr's Garage trying to find out about the brakes on Ms. Finch's car."

His face was beet red. Nelda couldn't tell if it was from the heat or from a temper tantrum he was having.

"Let me tell you something, Joe Coates. I don't work for you and I can durn well go and do as I please."

Nelda thought the sheriff was acting out his feelings of insecurity for not solving the mystery right away. She knew from experience some of these murder cases were long and drawn out. He'd better settle down and accept all the help he could get.

Joe sat silent for a minute. Nelda assumed he was thinking of how to respond to her act of independence. Finally, he spoke softly.

"I don't know how to talk to you, Nelda. It doesn't seem right that an officer of the law should need help from a citizen. I've always worked with just my men to solve a case. Somehow this case is different. My hands seem to be tied in this community. People don't trust someone they don't know."

This was the first time Joe had even hinted he needed her help; it was in her mind a real breakthrough. Just maybe they could work together.

"I trust you, Joe. Couldn't we be friends and help each other? I'm not going to stop investigating this murder. I want to find out who murdered Laura as much as you do."

A summer breeze blew in from the north as the sun sank in the west taking the temperature down with it. He rocked back and forth in the rocker as Nelda's metal chimes, hanging in an old oak tree, made melodious sounds. Finally, he stopped the rocking chair and spoke with just a suggestion of a smile on his lips.

"You win, Nelda. Let's exchange information?"

Nelda sank down on the steps. "I suppose my first question is why Edward and Thomas had a confrontation with Laura before she was killed. Did they own up to it?"

"Well, they certainly couldn't deny talking to her since everyone at the party saw and heard them in the shed."

"That's right. Edward was raising Cain. I think Thomas was just begging. So, what were their answers?" Nelda finally felt like she was getting somewhere.

"Her brother said he wanted her to lend him some money, and Thomas asked Laura to come back to work for his company."

Joe's answers were firm and precise, as though he hated to give out that information. Nelda was clearly disappointed with what she heard. It was certainly nothing new for Edward to beg for money, and it made sense that Thomas would want Laura back at work. These squabbles didn't add up to Laura's horrible death. She didn't know what she expected to hear.

"Another question, why did Laura quit her job? All she told me was she didn't like the procedures used." Nelda got up, stretched and swatted a mosquito on her arm.

Joe reluctantly warmed up to the conversation. "I'm no medical doctor, but according to Thomas, Laura thought the large amounts of hormones prescribed for young women selling their eggs for test-tube fertilization, was dangerous to their health."

Nelda leaned against a back-porch post and frowned. "For some reason Laura didn't want to tell me why she quit her job. She wouldn't discuss it with me." Nelda wondered to herself if the reason given by Thomas was the real reason.

It was growing late and she didn't want to miss her opportunity to talk to Antara. She rushed on with her next concern, knowing her turn to answer questions would be next. "Joe, why are you so certain that Max is the killer?"

"I'm not certain, but his fingerprints are on the box of poison and he had a motive."

"You mean because Laura's home was built on some property that used to belong to his father?"

"No, because the county road cut through their property. Laura's father was the engineer who helped build the road through Max's daddy's farm."

"That's so bizarre, to hold a grudge over that for all these years." Nelda doubted Max's involvement in the case, but she did realize the man was definitely strange, and would bear watching.

"I'm not quite sure he's the guilty party, but he's at the top of my list. But now it's your turn for answers, Nelda," Joe said, getting out of the rocker.

"Fire away," Nelda answered, thinking that she had very little to add about the case.

Joe walked out in the yard and looked at the pink sky in the west. "Did Laura tell you somebody was trying to kill her?"

Nelda was taken aback at the question. Now, she was caught. Joe must have sensed she knew something. She chewed on her lower lip and hated herself for what she was about to do.

"She did tell me that someone had tampered with her brakes causing her to hit a tree."

Joe gave Nelda a steady gaze, his pupils looked like pin size buoys on oceans of blue. "Did she say who that might be?"

Nelda was in despair. "I'm going to tell you what she told me, but you can't take any stock in it because Laura was emotionally distraught."

Joe leaned against a tree. His face was shadowed by a large branch over his head.

"Tell me about it," he said quietly.

"Laura bought her parents old home, and that's where she was living when she died. This house was badly burned on the inside twenty-three years ago. Her mother was killed in that fire and Laura feels responsible for setting it." She can't remember if she did or not."

"What does this have to do with someone trying to kill her now?"

"Just let me finish my story. She was sixteen when her mother died and now Antara is sixteen. When we were in New Orleans, Laura told me that Antara might be a bad seed. That maybe Antara had inherited the tendency to commit murder from her."

"Who's murder?"

"Laura's by cutting the brake hose." Nelda hung her head. She felt she was betraying her own flesh and blood. She just knew none of this was true.

Joe shook his head. "I'm sorry Nelda, but these woman with their over active imaginations are too much for me. All I deal with are facts, not fantasy."

Nelda trembled with relief. "I'm so happy to hear you say that. I'm sure Antara had nothing to do with the brake hose or her mother's death."

"What kind of relationship did these two have?"

"The kind that most parents have with teenagers, except there was no father around. This made it doubly hard for Laura to try and discipline her."

"Has she been in any scrapes with the law?" Joe asked.

"No, not that I know of. She makes good grades in school, but is having trouble growing up."

Joe came out from under the tree smiling. "I know some grownups like that. I'll try to talk to her before the week is out. I'd like her side of the story."

"I don't mean to rush you, Joe, but I've got to go out in a few minutes. Was there some other question you wanted to ask?"

"Guess not, Nelda. Now that we know we can talk to each other. Let's keep it up."

Nelda walked around to the front with him. The pink sky was fading as Swallowtail flycatchers swooped through the air scooping up mosquitoes. Nelda loved the twilight hour, but knew that enjoyment would have to wait. She'd have to hurry with her supper and bath to make it to the library by eight.

*   *   *

Nelda heard a terrible racket in the lane of traffic behind her car as she approached the City Library. She tried to locate the culprit filling the air with smoke and noise pollution by looking in her side mirror, but she was too far ahead to see who it was. Turning into the library parking lot, she scanned the parked cars to see if Mary's green Chevrolet was among the parked cars. Nelda couldn't find it. Good, Mary probably dropped Antara off and she'd get to talk to the young girl alone.

As she approached the library door, the man with the loud muffler and oil smoking truck pulled into the parking lot. Nelda couldn't suppress the urge to turn around. There was Max Beaux slouched behind the wheel. His bald head gleamed in the glow of a passing car's headlights. A cloud of blue smoke hung over the truck. *Nelda Sees Blue.*

Why was this strange old man following her?

CHAPTER FOURTEEN

The Stalker

Before entering the library, Nelda scanned the parking lot for Max Beaux. He and his smoking truck had disappeared. No use worrying needlessly, she thought; his appearance at the library might have some simple explanation. Perhaps he was meeting someone here. And yet, could it really be just a coincidence? She couldn't help being concerned for Antara. Max did blame her family for the loss of his father's farm.

The City Library was relatively new, all glass in front with a large lobby that opened up to a meeting room on the left. To the right were a book depository and rest rooms. An old man with mop in hand looked up as she passed through the lobby. He shoved a "wet floor" sign toward her, as though to announce it was almost closing time.

Suddenly, a hand touched her on the shoulder. She whirled around expecting to see an acquaintance, perhaps one of the students she'd taught before retiring. To her surprise Max Beaux stood in front of her grinning sheepishly. He had dressed in a faded plaid shirt and wrinkled blue jeans, looked as if he was ready to work in someone's garden.

"Howdy Ms. Simmons. You remember me, don't you?"

"I couldn't forget you. You and Dennis were out at my cousin's place the day she was poisoned."

Max twisted his Dallas Cowboy cap in his hands. "Yes Ma'am, I shore was there, but I ain't had nothing to do with that woman's death."

"What are you doing here?"

"Just 'cause I work with my hands don't mean I can't read," he answered in a belligerent tone.

"I'm sorry, Max. I didn't mean to give the impression you shouldn't be here. I guess I was just startled to see you."

"Mr. Toliver told me how you spy on people and get 'em into trouble. Just don't try it with me." His mood had turned sour, a complete personality change.

Before Nelda could respond, Max shoved the outside doors open and shuffled out into the night. He never looked back, just headed in the direction of a Shamrock station located next to the library. Nelda wanted to follow Max and talk about what was bothering him. But it was useless to follow him; he'd disappeared behind the cars.

Nelda hurried inside and stood at the information desk located in the center. From there she searched the long rows of library books and tables for a glimpse of Antara. Finally, she spotted her sitting at a table surrounded by mountains of books. She wasn't reading, but leaning on her elbows staring straight ahead as though deep in thought.

As Nelda approached, Antara saw her and smiled. The red rinse was fading from her black hair and without the spooky makeup she looked more like a young teen than a hooker. The resemblance to her dead mother was down right scary, even the same path of freckles on her right cheek.

"Thanks for coming, Nelda. You must think I'm screwy after the lie I told."

Nelda pulled a chair out and moved a mound of books out of the way so she could see Antara's face. From experience, she learned that you could usually tell if someone was telling the truth by looking into their eyes.

"I really didn't know what to make of it when you said you knew nothing about cars, especially with an "A" in auto mechanics."

Antara bit her bottom lip trying to keep back the tears. "I didn't know how to react when you asked me that. Of course I know something about the brakes on a car. I didn't want to admit it, though. You might have thought I was responsible for mother's car accident."

"Were you?" Nelda asked, giving her a steady gaze.

"Of course not! I really loved her and wish I'd been a better daughter."

Antara's nose leaked and tears cascaded down her cheeks. Nelda reached for a tissue, placed it in the girl's lap while trying to comfort her with some motherly pats.

"Antara, we can't undo the past, but you can become the daughter your mother wanted you to be."

61

"Oh Nelda, I hope you're right. I'm going to try. But please work hard on tracking down her killer." She ignored the tissue and wiped her face with the tail of her shirt.

"You know I will," smiled Nelda. "Now tell me everything you know about the people attending your birthday party."

Antara swallowed hard while gathering her thoughts. It seemed she didn't want to go back to that scene. Finally, shaking her head in resignation, she talked without looking directly at Nelda.

"Well, Derek wouldn't hurt a flea."

"How did he and your mom get along?"

"Super, he didn't like it when I was mean to her. He thought she was cool."

"How about your Uncle Edward."

"Now that's a whole new bag. Sometimes he looked at Mom like he wanted to kill her."

"What was the problem between them?"

"He thought she started the fire in my grandparents' home."

"What about your mom's inheritance from her parents? Did she ever discuss that with you in relation to your uncle?"

"No, she always said I'd be cared for if anything happened to her."

"And tell me about Thomas, why did your mom and Thomas break off their engagement."

"I don't know, but I'm sure Thomas loved her more than she loved him."

"What about her job. Why did she quit that?"

"I think it had something to do with her principles."

"What was the lab doing that she disapproved of?"

"Beats me. Mother and I didn't have discussions at our evening meals or, come to think about it, any other time."

"You didn't know Dennis, the yard man, or Max, his helper, very well did you?"

"Never saw them before they came to work for us. We had a neighbor's son cutting the grass, but Mom decided there was a lot more that needed to be done. That's why she contacted Dennis Toliver."

Mrs. Moore, an old librarian whom Nelda knew well, was flipping the light switch on and off in an effort to tell people it was time to go home. Her tired, blue eyes looked out from thick lenses and Nelda noticed she was favoring one foot. Time for us to leave and let her close up, thought Nelda.

"One more question. Your mother said she was going to a psychologist, who was it?"

"Her name is Shirley Long. Don't know if she was helping Mom or not."

Nelda jotted the name down in a little notebook she carried in her purse.

"How did you get here?" Nelda asked.

"With Derek, but Aunt Mary is picking me up in a few minutes."

"I'm glad we had this talk, Antara. The killer will be found and punished."

"I sure hope so. One thing Mother's death did bring about."

"What's that?"

"Me growing up a little. I've been so selfish and silly."

"Don't forget weird."

Antara laughed, causing Nelda to think the healing process had begun. Of course she didn't expect miracles too soon. Antara's fingernails were still sky blue, and Nelda hoped the small Monarch butterfly on the back of her hand was just a painting.

"I'll walk out with you when we put these books up," Nelda said.

"Thanks." Antara handed Nelda several books. One of them was titled, *"Genetic Patterns."*

Oh, thought Nelda, why is Antara reading that book? Surely Laura didn't tell her she was a bad seed and accuse her of tampering with her car.

"What's with this interest in genetics?" Nelda asked.

She gave Nelda a sardonic grin. "Well, Mom often said we were two peas in a pod. I just wanted to see which traits I might have inherited."

"I see." And Nelda did understand. She also wondered if Antara knew the identity of her father.

* * *

A few minutes later they were standing on the sidewalk outside the library waiting for Mary. Nelda exchanged greetings with Mary when she drove up, then walked to her own car. Stratus clouds had blocked out the moon, but the parking lights helped Nelda locate her Ford wagon. As Nelda left the parking lot, Mary drove her car into the street bound for home with Max's old smoke buggy right behind her. Nelda was amazed. She was right; he was following Antara.

This was one time Nelda wished she had invested in a cell phone. She just itched to call the sheriff and tell him all about this latest development. For all she knew Old Max could have flipped out. She would follow them to make sure he didn't get out of his truck after they got home.

A few blocks away Max turned down another street, but Nelda continued to follow Mary's car to make sure this was not a ruse he had pulled. She had to get this old man out of her hair. He was driving her nuts.

Ten minutes later Mary and Antara pulled up in their driveway without a hitch. There was no sound of Max's old jalopy, but Nelda wanted to make sure he didn't show up later. Without letting Mary or Antara know, she parked several houses away where she had a good view of their home. Nelda waited patiently to see what might develop, nothing did. She found herself dozing off after an hour and decided they were safe and wouldn't have any visitors.

Heading for home she played a Nat King Cole tape, singing along to one of her favorite songs, "Old Black Magic." She was almost there when she heard a fire truck siren behind her. Pulling over and coming to a stop, Nelda had goose bumps thinking of some poor family in trouble. It wasn't until she came to the end of the block where her large ancestral home was located that Nelda realized it was her home that was burning.

Knowing the firemen wouldn't let her get very close in her car, Nelda parked and started running toward her yard. Dark smoke was boiling out of the kitchen. She fought back the tears as neighbors stood in their driveways and called to her as she sped by.

Nelda rushed up to a fireman straightening a fire hose out in the street. He spoke to her without stopping his work. "Hey lady you can't get this close to the fire. You might get hurt."

"It's my house, mister. Does the fire seem very large?"

"I'm sorry lady, I just got here, but it seems to be confined to the kitchen. Now you best wait across the street till we put this out."

She joined Bess and Tom Howard in their yard across the street. "Did you turn the fire in, Tom?" Nelda asked.

"No, we were watching television and didn't see it until Bess heard the siren. We're sure sorry, but I think it's just the kitchen that caught fire."

Bess, dressed in a house dress and slippers, slipped an arm around Nelda. "Don't worry, Nelda, they'll have it out in no time. The greatest damage will probably be from the dirty feet of the firemen."

All those old treasures stored in her kitchen cabinets destroyed in just a few minutes. Nelda felt light headed and sat on the grass while Tom ran to get her a glass of water. She found herself looking for an old Chevy truck and the weathered face of a certain ex-con. There was no trace of either.

CHAPTER FIFTEEN

Invitation

Nelda woke up early. At first she didn't know where she was, then she recognized Sue's old, lumpy, brown hide-a-bed under her. What a night, her back hurt and her limbs were numb from sleeping in a cramped position. Then, she remembered the fire that destroyed her kitchen and all the lovely antique glassware stored in her cabinets. She sat straight up and let out a scream. Nelda beat the pillow with her fist.

Sue, half dressed, came running from the bathroom. "Aunt Nelda, what's wrong?"

"I just realized why I spent the night here."

"Your house was all smoky. You couldn't spend the night there."

"I still can't understand why anyone would want to burn my home. Could it be that awful, awful, old demented man?"

"Well, who else? I mean, he knew you were away from the house."

"I know, but he didn't have a reason for doing that unless he thought I was a threat."

"In his twisted mind, you probably are."

"Right now I'm a widow without a home. I've got to talk to the sheriff."

"You had two calls while you were sleeping, one from the sheriff and the other from Antara. I didn't want to wake you, so I told them you'd call them when you woke up."

Nelda yawned, stretched out her arms and looked down at the baby doll pajamas she'd borrowed from Sue. She couldn't help snickering as she looked at the brief underpants. Grabbing her own clothes, Nelda headed for the bedroom to dress.

She yearned for her early morning coffee and morning paper. No time this morning for those luxuries even if Sue owned a coffee pot or subscribed to the local paper (which she didn't).

While she dressed, the phone rang. It was the Finch's family lawyer, Robert Lavish. Sue handed Nelda the telephone.

"Nelda, heard about your fire on the news last night. I'm terribly sorry. How bad was it?"

"Thanks for thinking of me, Robert. The interior of the kitchen is in bad shape and the whole house is smoke damaged."

"Well listen, do you have some place to stay while the renovations are made?"

"Not really. Sue, of course will put me up, but she only has one bedroom. I'll probably find an apartment until the house is restored." Nelda couldn't imagine why Robert was interested in her interim stay unless he had some rent property.

"You know Laura's house is empty and we've been notified that the fire insurance will be canceled unless someone is living there. Antara called me after she heard about your fire. She asked me to invite you to live there until your house is livable."

"Really, how kind of her. You mean she wants me to rent it?" Nelda was wondering if her budget could afford it.

"No, you'll be doing her a favor. Realtors will be showing it of course. I hope you don't mind that."

"No, that's fine. I'll call you after I talk with Antara and Mary."

Nelda said good-bye and hung up. The thought of staying in the Old Finch House gave her chill bumps. She supposed it was because two family members who had lived in the house had violent deaths: Laura's mother, Irene, when the house was set on fire, and now Laura from poison. But it was foolish to blame their deaths on that lovely old homestead.

* * *

Sue needed a ride to work. "Your car is always on the blink, Sue," Nelda said with some irritation. She loved her niece, but car maintenance was not one of Sue's long suits.

"Don't be mad, Aunt Nelda, my old Pacer is just worn out. If I could afford the payments, I'd get a new one in a heartbeat, but I can't."

Nelda was instantly sorry for her sharp remark. Sue couldn't help herself. She was an excellent nurse, but mechanical things were just beyond her ability to understand.

"Well, don't worry about your car. I'm sure it just needs some little part."

Sue relaxed a little and smiled. "What are you going to do with Sally when she gets here?"

Nelda put a hand to her forehead. "I forgot that she's coming for a visit."

Sally and Nelda went way back. Sally Feddington had been the senior English teacher at the school where Nelda taught science, but now Sally had retired to the country. The two old friends still maintained a close relationship.

"Too late to call her now! I'm sure she's already on her way." Like Nelda, Sally was an early riser, and when she had some place to go she liked to start out at the crack of dawn.

"You know both of you can bunk in my apartment."

Nelda winced as she remembered the brown sofa. "Thanks, Sue, but I might take the offer made by Robert Lavish. He said Antara suggested I stay in the old homestead, which she now owns, until repairs are made to my house. I don't think she would mind if Sally stayed with me for awhile."

"Great idea."

"And I tell you, I would feel a lot safer having someone with me at night if I stayed out there. Two family deaths associated with that house make me nervous."

"Pooh, Aunt Nelda, next thing you know you'll be having all the ghosts exorcised from it. This is really not like you."

"You're right," said Nelda, pulling into the parking lot of the clinic where Sue worked. "I guess the fire and no sleep has me a little rattled.

"Are you going home to meet Sally?" Sue asked, getting out of the station wagon.

"First, I'm going to talk to the sheriff and then I'll go to my house and wait for her. I'll have plenty to keep me busy. I just hope I can salvage some of the things in the kitchen."

"Call me later and let me know your plans for tonight. I'll get a ride home." Sue threw Nelda a kiss.

Before Nelda drove out of the clinic parking lot she pulled out a compact and freshened her makeup. There was nothing she could do to make her hair look better. Tossing and turning on the sofa had given it a feathery look. Oh well, she reasoned; Joe Coates has seen hen feathers before. He's a country boy. It surprised her that she would even care how she looked. She was sure the sheriff was just a bull headed man who thought women had no place in crime investigations.

The drive to the sheriff's office took only a few minutes. She had not called him back as he requested, because she found interviews in person yielded more information than over the phone. Surely he would be able to tell her how the fire started.

Sentiment overcame her as she drove into the shaded parking area next to the sheriff's office. For thirty years she'd visited this place to help her husband, Jim, solve crimes. He had been the sheriff until his death several years ago. Times were hard in the county when he first started. There was no way to pay for a deputy. Working for the thrill of it was how she got paid for being his assistant. It was an adventure for both of them. Now, she wondered how she had juggled her teaching career and the detective work. Nelda wiped a tear away. She didn't have time to reminisce, there was a crime to solve.

As she approached the building, she could have sworn someone was watching her from behind the venetian blind. Maybe Joe had a habit of watching out his window or maybe she was good at digging up old ghosts.

As Nelda entered the building she stopped to chat with the sheriff's secretary, Vera. It felt just like old times.

"Nelda, it's so good to see you. Haven't seen much of you since our young sheriff went off to school."

"I know, and I miss coming here too. That temporary sheriff isn't expecting me. Could you let him know I'm here?"

"He's ahead of you; he saw you coming. Just go on in."

Well, so much for old ghosts, Nelda thought. Hope he'll tell me all he knows about my fire. She knocked on his door, and a few seconds later Joe was holding it open for her.

"Nelda, come in and sit down. I'm glad you decided to visit me instead of telephoning,"

69

She sat in a chair opposite his desk and noticed how neat and orderly everything was. And then something wonderful materialized right under her nose. It was a fresh brewed cup of coffee.

"How did you know I missed my coffee this morning? It smells wonderful."

Joe grinned as Nelda doctored her coffee with cream and sugar. Being a coffee lover, he understood her craving very well.

"I know you spent the night with Sue, and the majority of young people don't drink coffee."

"Sue used to love it, but found out it made her very nervous. Now she doesn't even own a coffee pot."

"Too bad. Guess you're wondering what we found out about last night."

"That was going to be my next question," said Nelda, taking a big sip from her cup.

Joe began to pace. "It was the strangest thing, the arsonist had it all planned. It wasn't something done on the spur of the moment. Someone took a stack of newspapers, put them in the middle of your kitchen and started a fire."

Nelda put her cup down. "Those newspapers came from my utility room. I stack them there and then turn them in for recycling. What did he use for fuel?"

"A five-hundred milliliter test tube was filled with gasoline. It was stoppered with a cloth and thick string was used as a wick. The perpetrator laid a trail with the wick to the back window of your kitchen. He undoubtedly soaked the wick in gasoline first."

"He used the wick so he wouldn't be there when the papers started burning," Nelda said, holding up her cup for a refill.

"You bet. We've identified the ash from the wick and stopper as cotton. The test tube was unbroken and taken in as evidence. We haven't a clue as to who did it."

"How did he get into the house? The back window was locked."

"He broke one of the panes, then reached in unlocked the window and pushed it up."

"Any fingerprints, or eye witnesses?

"Afraid not. I'm sure he wore some type of gloves and as for the neighbors seeing, you do have a big lot with a privacy fence and quite a collection of well cared for tall plants."

"That's true. I never thought I'd have to worry about too much privacy."

Nelda noticed that Joe had circles under his eyes and he rubbed his temples as though his head ached. His uniform was neat as ever and it looked like he'd just polished his boots, but he just didn't exude the energy she'd encountered in their last meeting.

"When we talked yesterday evening, Nelda, you said you were going out. Who else knew you weren't going to be home?"

"Right after you left, I went to the library to visit Antara. After I got to the library, Max Beaux pulled into the parking lot. I don't know if he was following me or not."

"Well, why was he at the library?" Joe looked puzzled.

"My thoughts exactly," said Nelda putting her cup down. "I actually asked him that question and he took offense to it. I thought it was odd that he would be there at the very same time Antara and I were there."

"What exactly did he say?"

Nelda thought a minute. "I don't know his exact words, but he said he could read and had a right to be there. He also accused me of stirring up trouble for people."

Joe sat down heavily. "Who gave him that idea?"

"He said it came from Dennis, but I know it's not so. Dennis and I are old friends. In fact, Dennis was one of my high school students."

"Sue told me that when Antara and her aunt left the library parking lot that Max followed them," Joe said.

"I thought he was following them, but he turned off on another street before they got home. That's why I parked a half block down from Mary's house to see if he would show up."

Joe rubbed his big hands together. "Why didn't you call me and let me know what was going on?"

Nelda squirmed in her seat and rubbed her sore shoulder. "I didn't know anything was going on and wasn't near a phone."

"You mean to tell me you run around at night without a car phone? Nelda, you need a phone for protection."

"I've gotten along fine without a car phone for all these years." Nelda said stubbornly.

Joe got up abruptly and stood by the window. "I don't think Max started the fire."

"You don't? Why not?"

"The man is a little strange, but he's crafty. Maybe, just maybe, it's a frame job. And if the arsonist had really wanted to destroy your house there would have been a lot more damage."

Nelda got up to leave. She had her doubts about Max being Lara's murderer too. "You do have several other suspects," she said.

"Yes, and I haven't much to show for all the investigating I've been doing."

Empathy washed over Nelda. How many times had she been in this same situation. The answers to most mysteries didn't come easily.

"Don't worry. Things will work out. Before I go I'd like to tell you where I'll be living for the next month or so."

"While your house is repaired?"

"Yes, Antara has invited me to live in her old homestead. I'm going to take her up on the offer."

"That's so far out. Will you stay there alone?" Joe's face was creased with concern.

"My friend, Sally Feddington, is coming for a visit and she'll be with me for a while. I might talk her into staying the whole time." Nelda walked to the door.

Joe opened the door for her. "That's good. If I find out anything new about the fire I'll let you know. Oh and, Nelda, one other thing."

"What's that?" Nelda asked.

"Edward Finch has moved back to town."

Nelda's eyes opened wide. "And what is he doing here?"

Joe watched the expression on Nelda's face with interest. "He's working for the Cisco Chemical Plant."

CHAPTER SIXTEEN

Thomas's Secrets

That was interesting news from Joe about Edward, Nelda thought as she drove home. Now all the suspects in Laura's death lived in one area, and they knew where she lived too. Didn't they all have access to large test tubes such as the one used to start the fire? Edward is now working for a chemical company. Thomas has a laboratory and Max could have bought one at the Producers Co-op. She shook her head at the complexity of it all. Having Sally around would be a treat. It was nice to have someone she could trust to hear her speculations concerning the case. Sally was a wonderful sounding board.

Nelda mused over her last case involving a murdered doctor. She and Sally were almost killed in a sabotaged car, but both of them kept their sense of humors. Now Nelda needed fun and a little entertainment to keep her sanity. Bad events were happening too frequently.

Even as she neared her home the signs of a fire were obvious. Smoke had painted the white planks on the exterior kitchen walls black. She pulled up in the driveway and was hesitant to open the door. All the beautiful plants she'd planted to attract butterflies and humming birds were sadly trampled by the fire fighters. Snapdragons, Sweet William, and Hollyhocks needed replanting.

When she first entered the house, she could barely smell smoke, but as she walked down the hall to the kitchen the odor caused Nelda to bring out her handkerchief and cover her nose. She held her breath as she looked toward the cabinet that housed her Copenhagen Mother's Day Plates. The cabinet door was missing, and fragments of the plates were scattered all over the kitchen. The ones not destroyed by fire had been broken by the firemen in their attempt to put out the flames.

Suddenly, there were footsteps in the hall. Nelda's heart beat faster. She hid in the utility room next to the kitchen.

"Oh my Lord," squeaked a voice that Nelda couldn't help recognizing as Sally's. She peeked out at her friend, who was

73

shaking her gray head from side to side. The lenses of Sally's glasses reflected the mess on the kitchen floor.

"Sally, you scared me half to death, but I'm so happy to see you." Nelda embraced the short, chubby woman.

"You left the door open, so I came on in. What happened here, Nelda?"

"A fire last night. I tried to call you this morning, but you were already on the road."

"I can't stand the smell of smoke, and the sight of all your ruined antiques. I'll see you outside." Sally ran down the hall holding her nose.

"I'll meet you in a few minutes," Nelda called as Sally disappeared.

Nelda approached the closet off the kitchen with dreaded concern. If anything had happened to her old comic book collection, she didn't know what she'd do. After taking a cardboard box out of the closet, she removed the lid and breathed a sigh of relief. The comic books stored inside were in perfect condition. They were from her *Catwoman* collection. "Thank you," she whispered, looking up at the heavens. With moist eyes she picked up the box and joined Sally on the front porch.

Sally asked, "What caused the fire?"

"It was deliberately set," answered Nelda.

"Oh no!" Sally whispered, "Who did it?"

"We don't know yet. I thought you'd have to turn around and go home, but Antara invited me to stay in Laura's house. Would you like to spend a few days with me while my house is being repaired?"

"That's where Laura was poisoned, wasn't it?" Sally sounded frightened.

"Yes, and Antara has it for sale. I'm fortunate they asked me to live there, because I can't stay in my house with all that smoke damage."

"Laura's house is way out in the country."

"It's out of the city limits, yet in twenty minutes you can be shopping in town."

"I know you need someone to stay with you, so I'll do it. You need some protection. What about Sugar? I could go get him."

Nelda couldn't help laughing. Sugar, Sally's old brown Labrador, was a major player in the last mystery. He didn't do anything to help, but got them in a lot of trouble when he ran away.

"No, please, not now. We may be out most of the time and not able to care for him."

Sally agreed that Sugar was with a neighbor who loved him. If they didn't need him here, he would be better off with her friend.

"I'll put my comic book collection on the back seat and then we'll have lunch at The Green Shepherd. We've got a lot to talk about."

"That sounds like a vegetarian restaurant, is it?" Sally pointed a pudgy finger at Nelda.

"Just get in the car. We'll pick up your car after lunch. You're going to love the food. Your arteries will love it too." Nelda was enjoying Sally's negative reaction to her restaurant selection.

Sally got in beside Nelda and buckled up. "You're always trying to make me eat less fat, Nelda, however I'm doomed. Nonfat foods have no taste. It's kind of like eating sawdust."

"I know you've eaten a lot of wood in your day," Nelda teased as she drove down the street.

"I don't know. They're always changing their minds as to what's good for you. Remember when eating an egg was a no no, and now one a day doesn't hurt you."

"You're right. You just have to use common sense."

Nelda entertained Sally by describing her night on Sue's old couch. They were both laughing when they pulled in the parking lot at the Green Shepherd. Although it was only eleven, the parking lot was almost full.

"Hey," Sally said. "This place must be pretty good."

"Really good," Nelda answered scrutinizing the cars in the parking lot.

"Now I get it, someone is here you want to talk to about Laura's death."

"Am I that easy to read?" smiled Nelda. "That black Volvo belongs to Thomas Compton. Laura was engaged to him and broke it off before she died."

"How did you know he'd be here?"

"Laura told me he ate an early lunch in this restaurant almost every day. Lets go in and find a table."

After entering the restaurant, they had no trouble finding a place to sit. The restaurant contained numerous booths plus a few tables for large groups. The interior was like being in a garden. Many plants adorned the floor, hung from the ceiling and were placed on dividers between the booths. Nelda loved it, but Sally began to rub her nose.

"Oh, I hope I'm not allergic to any of these plants." She pushed the broad leafed fern on the ledge toward Nelda's side.

They looked up to see one of their students, Gail Beasley, waiting tables. She was a vivacious girl with black, curly hair and a mouth that never stopped talking. Gail spotted them, then tripped over a red begonia before making it over to their booth.

"This is my day. My two favorite teachers." Gail hugged them.

"Glad you didn't break your neck on that plant," Sally said.

"Isn't this place a hoot? We have fifty varieties of plants in here."

"That's terrific," exclaimed Nelda. "How long have you had this job?"

"Since it opened six months ago. My uncle owns the joint, a family thing you know."

"I've eaten in here several times, but didn't see you."

"Going to Smitherton Junior College at night."

"Good for you." Nelda turned to Sally. "Let's try the Green Shepherd Special: four vegetables, rolls, herb tea and fruit yogurt dessert."

"Sounds yummy," said Sally sarcastically.

"You'll love it," Nelda nodded at Gail.

They made their selection of vegetables. Nelda choose green beans, mashed potatoes, black eyed peas and squash. Sally moaned, but finally choose fried okra, egg plant, hash brown potatoes and carrots.

"Is that it? You ladies are easy to please,"

"One other thing," said Nelda. "You must know Thomas Compton if you've been working here ever since it opened. Could you tell me where he's sitting?"

"The poor thing, he looks so lonesome," said Gail. "He hunkers down in the same spot he used to sit in with Laura Finch. You know the woman who was poisoned?"

"And where might that spot be?"

"In the booth next to the rest rooms. There's a giant spiderwort plant hanging over his head."

After they ordered, Nelda excused herself to go to the rest room. Sally smiled knowingly and watched her walk away. When Nelda approached the booth with the spiderwort plant overhead, she found it empty. She couldn't believe she'd missed him. How could he get by them without being seen? Was he hiding from her?

"Nelda," said a voice behind her. She whirled to find Thomas still drying his hands on a piece of paper towel.

"I was looking for you, Thomas, glad you're still here."

He wore a freshly ironed plaid shirt with navy blue pants. Even though he was neatness personified, Nelda wished he would get a little sun. His pale skin and thin, blonde hair gave him an unhealthy appearance.

"Well, how in the world did you know I'd be here?" His voice sounded suspicious of her sudden appearance.

"Laura told me you ate here every day."

Nelda witnessed a complete change in Thomas's facial expression. His mouth tightened and his eyes became moist. He removed his gold rimmed glasses and rubbed his eyes.

"I'm sorry, Thomas. It must be tough remembering her. I loved her too. Would you like to come over and eat with me and my friend?"

"That would be nice, Nelda." He went back to the booth to retrieve a large black briefcase. "And I just want to say I'm sorry about your house. I heard about it on TV this morning."

"Thank you," said Nelda leading the way back to her booth.

When they arrived, Nelda introduced Sally. "Thomas, this is my dear friend, Sally Feddington. We taught school together for years and now we've retired together."

Thomas smiled at Sally, but did not shake her outstretched hand. "It's good to meet you. Thank you both for allowing me to join you."

They settled in the booth and visited while they waited for their food to arrive. Nelda didn't quite know how to get Thomas, the reserved scientist, to talk. Showing an interest in his successful clinic might open him up.

"How is your practice going, Thomas?" Nelda asked.

"Fine, just fine. I sure miss having Laura at the clinic." His eyes narrowed as he looked at Nelda. "Did she ever tell you why she quit her job?"

"No, she didn't." Nelda could swear he looked relieved.

"We didn't see eye to eye on some policies I have in place there. I couldn't change them for her. But what about your house? Will you be able to live in it while it's being repaired?"

Nelda could see he didn't want to discuss Laura's involvement with his clinic. She was sorry about that. She'd have to find out why Laura quit some other way.

"No," she said to his question. "I'll have to find temporary accommodations."

Their food arrived. Gail, realizing that Thomas had moved, brought his salad over to their booth. Nelda was delighted that Sally didn't turn up her nose at the vegetables, but wolfed them down just as she did. Thomas, on the other hand, just picked at his Caesar salad and crunched on some bread sticks. For some reason he had no appetite.

"I've always been fascinated with fertility clinics," said Sally. Do you suppose Nelda and I could tour yours some day?"

Thomas put his hands together. They reminded Nelda of a teepee. His fingers were incredibly long and impeccably clean. He answered, after giving much thought to Sally's question.

"Friday is a good time to tour the clinic. We have no patients then. Maybe we could explain how we do our work."

Nelda looked at Sally in amazement. Here she was agonizing about how to get into the clinic when Sally simply asks for an invitation and received one. She felt like hugging her right then.

"That's a great idea, Sally." Nelda said. "Just think of all the women they have helped to have children."

Too late for me, thought Nelda. She and Jim would have loved to have had a child, but it didn't happen. As for Sally, she'd never married and probably had no interest in the clinic at all. She'd finagled that invitation for me, bless her heart.

"Well ladies, I'll leave you over your tea." Thomas picked up his briefcase. "I must get back to the clinic. I'll pay on the way out."

"Do you have a business card, Thomas? I'll call if we can visit next Friday."

Thomas set his briefcase on the table, and got a card out of his billfold. He handed it to Nelda then scurried out of the building.

"I hate to say this, Nelda, but he doesn't seem to have much of a personality. What do you suppose attracted Laura to him?"

"I suppose they both had biological backgrounds, or maybe she just liked the reserved, quiet kind of guy. What bugs me is why she changed her mind about marrying him."

"When do we move into Laura's house?" Sally asked, finishing her tea.

"I'll call Antara this afternoon, as soon as I get home. I've got to pack a bag and make sure my silver is in a safe place."

She signaled for Gail to bring the check. They walked to the cashier and both paid with big bills. Nelda went back to the booth to leave a tip. As she left a couple of dollars under the wine list, her eyes focused on a dark smear. She rubbed her finger across the tablecloth where Thomas had rested his briefcase. When she picked up her hand, there was something black on her fingers. It looked like, could it be soot?

CHAPTER SEVENTEEN

Settling In

Nelda still had the black substance on her fingers when she met Sally outside. "Do you see what's on my fingers?" Nelda asked, sticking her hand in front of Sally's face.

"Are you giving the restaurant a glove test?" Sally asked.

"No, this came off of Thomas Compton's briefcase when he put it down on the table. I think it's soot."

"You're kidding! He doesn't look like he'd want to dirty himself by starting fires."

"Well, what if Thomas wanted Max to take the blame for Laura's death."

"How would burning your house do that?" Sally asked.

"Max went to prison for burning houses. He thought the people who owned those homes were responsible for his daddy losing the family farm. You see, the farm was condemned by emminent domain for a county road. Sheriff Coates might think the vendetta goes on against relatives of Laura's father. Her father was the engineer that helped build the road."

"So, if Max could be blamed for Laura's death, this would stop the investigation."

"Of course, but the killer has to be running scared if he's trying to frame Max." Nelda looked at her watch. "Oh my goodness, we've got to get moving. I didn't realize the time. The painter is supposed to be at my house in fifteen minutes, and I have to make some calls while I'm there."

"If you had a cell phone, you wouldn't have to go in that smoky house."

"Not you too. The sheriff just got through lambasting me because I didn't have a phone. I suppose you have one?"

"Of course, but there would be a roaming fee if you used mine. And besides you know the sheriff is right."

Nelda grumbled under her breath as they buckled up. Life was getting too complicated. There were computer programs she needed to learn, and now she was outdated because she didn't have a cell phone. Toting a phone around with her would be equivalent to wearing a bell around her neck. Everyone would know where she was.

Sally prattled all the way back. Maybe they could see a play or go to the Chorale Concert, where they could hear music from the 40's and 50's.

"Nelda, you haven't heard a word I've said."

"Yes, I have. It's just that I've got a lot on my mind, all those phone calls, then the packing. It will be late afternoon before we can settle in Laura's house."

"That's fine with me, but let's not go after dark. What about the utilities?" She rubbed her arms as if she were cold.

"I'm sure they wouldn't offer me the house if the utilities were turned off," Nelda said as she turned down her street. "We'll get everything squared away when I call Antara."

A white van was parked in front of her house when she pulled up in the driveway. She recognized the driver as Sam Godfrey.

"Thank Goodness, there's the painter. I hope he can start working on the house right away. He does some carpentry work too."

They got out of the car and waited for Sam to join them. He was a tall, bald guy with two teeth missing in front. His overalls were speckled with several colors of paint, making him look like he'd been rolled in confetti.

"Hello Ms. Simmons. Sure am sorry about your house. Golly, all that soot, it's not a pretty sight." He made a hissing sound when he talked as though the words were pushed out through the opening made by his missing teeth.

"No it's not, Sam, but I know you can remedy that. By the way, this is my friend Sally Feddington."

"Oh, I know Miss Feddington. She is picky, picky when it comes to colors." After he spoke, he laughed, showing a wad of tobacco in his jaw.

Nelda promised herself to talk to Sam about his habit when she had the opportunity.

"I'm not picky," Sally shot back. "You just can't tell what color the paint is until it's on your wall. I just happened to change my mind a couple of times."

Nelda was in a hurry and didn't want to chitchat with Sam. "Well look, Sam, just paint everything its original color and you can't go wrong. Whatever is burned, replace it. My insurance company has okayed the repairs."

"I'll do my best, Ms. Simmons, but it'll take several weeks."

Nelda nodded. "Just move as fast as you can."

"I shore will. I'll start tomorrow if it's clear."

"Great, I'll be checking in with you from time to time. Remember to keep things locked up." She handed him the labeled keys to the front and back door.

"You can trust me." He placed the keys carefully in his pocket.

Sam waved good-bye to them as he slammed the door on his van and backed out.

"You really can trust him with the things in your home, Nelda. He's an honest man."

"I know he is and my neighbors are on alert too. Do you want to stay out here while I pack and make some calls?"

"I'll just sit on your front porch and be a bird watcher." As she spoke a blue jay chased a cardinal out of a bird feeder, but two Inca doves paid no attention to the noisy intruder.

Nelda was feeling somewhat better about her situation. She first called Antara, only to learn she was still in school. Mary, however, explained where the extra key was hidden, and assured Nelda that the utilities were still connected.

She hesitated about calling the sheriff. Was the soot on the briefcase worthy of suspicion? She had to say yes and made the call. The sheriff's secretary buzzed his office.

"Joe Coates here," was his gruff greeting.

"It's me, Nelda. I want to report something that might be related to my fire, but I'm not sure it has any significance at all."

"Glad you called, Nelda. I'll be happy to hear about anything you've discovered. My information so far is mighty scarce."

"My friend, Sally and I had lunch in the Green Shepherd restaurant today with Ned Compton. When he got ready to leave, he put his briefcase down on the table to give me a business card. I discovered soot on the tablecloth after he picked up his briefcase."

"So you think he might have started the fire and some of the soot was carried out on his briefcase?"

"I know that sounds far-fetched. I'm sure there were other ways for the soot to get there." Nelda felt foolish for taking up the sheriff's time. He must be laughing at her now.

"It's not far-fetched at all. I don't suppose you saved the tablecloth?"

"No," laughed Nelda, "but I do have my napkin with the soot on it. It's in a baggy."

"Great, it might be useful. Could you drop it off tomorrow?"

"Sure. Sally and I will be staying in the old Finch homestead for a while. If you want to contact me, call Laura's number."

"I'm glad you'll have someone with you. I don't have to tell you to lock your doors. There aren't any close neighbors."

"I know, thanks for your concern."

After she hung up, Nelda stared into space. You know, she thought, just maybe there is a heart under all that tough skin.

*   *   *

It was late afternoon when she and Sally arrived, in separate cars, at Laura's home. They'd stopped for groceries on the way. They both parked in the circular drive to unload. The old log house, with peeling paint, looked more neglected than ever. The ferns hanging on the front porch had turned brown from lack of water, and dust covered the grandfather rocking chairs. Shadows from the great oak trees gave the house an eerie appearance. Nelda looked around at Sally to see her reaction to the neglected place.

"Who's going to buy this dismal place, Nelda? The grounds are in terrible condition."

"You've got to see beyond that, Sally. If I didn't have my old homestead, I'd consider buying it. There are five beautiful acres here and the house is not in bad shape."

Sally shook her head. "This place gives me the willies."

Helen Sheffield

Nelda put her hand in the wire basket holding a Boston fern. She jumped back when a small wren flew out of the fern. After a little more searching, she came up with the front door key.

"My goodness, that bird gave me a start, but now we can get inside." Nelda held up the key. She couldn't wait to see Sally's reaction to all the lovely antiques inside.

The door opened easily and Nelda waited for Sally to enter. Then she stepped in and turned on the light. Sally gasped in amazement.

"I can't believe my eyes. All these beautiful antiques. I hope Antara hangs on to them." She headed toward the walnut china cabinet to inspect its contents.

Nelda watched Sally, a little smile playing on her lips. "There's no time for inspecting the antiques now. Let's put our things in the bedrooms upstairs, then go to he library."

"What on earth for? Can't we just sit down and relax for a little while?"

Nelda was ashamed of herself. She'd had Sally going all day after her long trip to Stearn. Maybe her friend did need a little time to relax and visit. Besides, the library was open until 9:00 p.m.

"Let's take our luggage upstairs, Sally, and I'll make us a cup of green tea and some chicken salad sandwiches."

Sally picked up her bag. "What about all those coffee beans you used to grind? A cup of coffee sure would taste good."

"I haven't given them up, just don't drink as many cups of coffee. Green tea has all kinds of good stuff in it, like antioxidants. It's good for you, even tastes good."

Nelda headed upstairs. She'd take Antara's room, to keep Sally from being really shocked. Oh my, miracles never cease to happen, she said to herself after pushing the bedroom door open. The place was in apple pie order, probably due to Mary's house cleaning magic. She looked under the bed to see if all the dirty towels and clothes had been removed. They had. Of course the things left behind were shocking enough, zebra design bedspread, rug and chair, but all signs of a messy teenager were gone. She breathed a sigh of relief and plopped on the bed. Oh, no, the teenage idol on roller blades, Mike Damus, still smiled down at her from the ceiling. Nelda grinned. Nice payback for her being such a square.

"Sally," Nelda called down the hall. "Are you doing okay?" How does your room suit you."

Sally stuck her head out the door. "This guest room is really something. It's entirely furnished with antiques. How about yours?"

Nelda laughed. "I'm the only antique in this room. It used to be Antara's bedroom. You ready for tea and a sandwich?"

"Yes, and while you boil the water I'll get the groceries out of your car."

"Great," Nelda said as she removed the tea from her suitcase and went down the stairs.

You couldn't tell the sheriff had investigated a murder in this kitchen. Everything was immaculate. Nelda opened up the cabinets and found no trace of the glasses or pitcher that were used to serve the lemonade on that fateful day. Even the sugar bowl and canister were empty, which was all right with Nelda. She didn't relish the idea of using anything that resembled strychnine crystals.

The kettle was sitting on the stove. She rinsed it thoroughly, filled it with water and set it back down on a lighted burner. The tea was ready by the time Sally came in with the two bags of groceries. They unloaded the bags and stored the groceries before taking their cups of green tea and chicken salad sandwiches into the living room. Each sat down with a sigh.

As Nelda set her cup on the coffee table, she noticed a large picture album with a delicate silver filigree of a young girl on its cover. It was exquisite.

"Look at this, Sally. I don't remember seeing this before." She picked up the album and opened it. To her surprise all the pictures were of Antara, or were they? The face was right, but the clothes were all wrong. The clothes and hair style were from the 60's.

Sally moved closer to have a look. "Those pictures are of Laura when she was a young girl."

"And how do you know that?" Nelda asked, while pulling her reading glasses out of her pocket.

"Because it says so on the labels under the pictures. Put your glasses on."

Nelda slipped her glasses on and eagerly read all the labels. "Antara is the spitting image of her mother at that age. Isn't it strange that they also had the same temperament?"

"Well, since you don't know the father, all you have to compare her with is her mother." Sally ran her hand over the cover appreciatively.

"You're right. Maybe the mother and father both had impulsive personalities. Antara will mature in time."

The grandfather clock in the hall chimed seven times. Sally looked at Nelda. "If we're going to the library, we better get going."

"Got your second wind back, huh? I was about to say let's just wait until tomorrow. We'll be fresher and can think better."

"Why were we going?" Sally asked. "I'm sure it has something to do with Laura's death, but tell me what you expect to find."

"We're going to search the local newspapers and find out everything we can about the arson cases in Stearn twenty-three years ago."

Hearing footsteps outside, Nelda put up her finger to silence Sally. Someone was prowling around outside. She motioned for Sally to leave the room, then grabbed a poker from the fireplace and turned out the light. As soon as she positioned herself behind the door, someone knocked with a heavy object. Goose bumps formed on Nelda's arms. Should she answer the door? The pounding continued only this time it was accompanied by a voice.

"Open up, I know you're in there."

The voice sounded angry. Nelda turned on the porch light and peeked through the curtained window. It was Edward holding a golf club in his hand. She turned the inside lights back on and opened up the door. Edward was shocked to see her. He was dressed in blue jeans, blue plaid shirt and wore gloves. It was that old blue danger signal again. *Nelda Sees Blue.*

CHAPTER EIGHTEEN

Unexpected Company

Edward placed the golf club on the porch rail as he peered in at Nelda. "What are you doing here?"

Nelda walked out on the porch. She looked at Edward's truck in the drive by the side of the house. It was loaded with Laura's patio table and chairs. "I could ask you the same question."

Edward looked back at his truck. "Antara gave me the patio furniture. You drove up while I was loading it. I thought you were a real estate agent showing the house, but then I realized you'd been in the house too long for that. Somehow suspicions about robbery got the better of me. The only weapon I could think of was my golf club." He smiled sheepishly.

Nelda relaxed a little with that information. "Yes, I can see why you thought there might be intruders. Now I'll answer your question. Antara invited me to live here until my house is repaired. You know about my fire don't you?"

"I heard about it. Aren't you afraid to go off and leave your home unguarded? Somebody might come back and finish the job."

"Lord, I hope not, but it's just a chance I'll have to take. My neighbors are on the lookout for strangers."

"Well, good luck." He picked up his golf club and turned to go.

Nelda wanted to delay Edward's departure. She needed to find out about his new job. "My friend, Sally, and I are having a sandwich and tea. Would you care to join us?"

"I'll pass on the sandwich and tea, but a Coke would be nice if you have one."

Edward walked into the room, and sat down gingerly on an antique chair. Nelda left to get his drink. On the way to the kitchen she passed Sally in the hall and whispered to her that the crisis was over. Sally made her way into the living room.

"Hello, Sally," Edward said as he stood up. "It's been awhile since I've seen you."

Helen Sheffield

"Sure has," answered Sally. "I guess it was at Laura's graduation from college."

Nelda came back with the drink and handed it to Edward, then they all sat down.

"Tell me, how is your new job going?" Nelda asked.

Edward's eyebrows shot up. "Nothing gets by you does it? I like my job fine. Had to leave a few treasures behind when I left the big city, but I'm sure I'll find some rough diamonds here."

Nelda supposed he was talking about girls, but she stayed with the job topic. "I didn't know you had a chemical background."

Edward laughed. "You don't have to be a chemist to sell chemical supplies, just a good salesman."

"You always were a smooth talker," Nelda conceded.

Sally couldn't keep quiet any longer. "Edward, are you going to let your old homestead get away from you?"

"Believe me, I wouldn't have this place, too many bad memories. And as for this furniture, it reminds me of a museum. It's not even comfortable." He wiggled in the chair causing the legs to creak.

Sally shook her head at his lack of appreciation for the fine old antiques, while Nelda took over the conversation.

"Edward, on the coffee table we found this picture album of Laura as a young girl." She picked up the album. "Antara's resemblance to her mother is uncanny."

Nelda held the book for Edward to see the pictures. As she turned the pages, a small, clear plastic bag filled with hair fell to the floor. A note was attached. She picked it up and read aloud, "Laura's hair pulled out by our old dog, Pug."

He laughed out-loud. "I was there when it happened. Laura was about two years old. She pulled on old Pug's ears all the time. One day he'd had enough, so he reached up and grabbed her hair. She had a bald spot from that little episode. I suppose mother thought the event was worth remembering."

As Edward looked at the pages of the album, his demeanor changed. His eyes took on a haunted look. "I've got to go, Nelda. It was good visiting with you and Sally. I apologize for giving you a scare by beating on the door." He abruptly stood up.

"We forgive you. No harm done."

88

"I've bought a condominium right up the road in Smitherton. I'm not quite squared away, but I'm getting there."

Sally took the glasses and plates to the kitchen while Nelda walked out on the porch with Edward. He stopped and spoke to her in a low voice.

"I know I'm a suspect in Laura's death because I inherited money that would have gone to her. But I tell you, Nelda, I had nothing to do with her death."

"Everyone at the party is a suspect," Nelda replied.

"I suppose so, some more than others, wouldn't you say?"

"Yes," Nelda said sitting on the porch rail. Her feet hurt and she wished he'd leave so she could take off her shoes.

"I've mixed feelings about my sister, and I'll tell you why."

All at once Nelda felt no pain in any part of her body. She braced herself for information that might further the investigation. "Tell me," she answered.

"When our home, and I mean this house, was gutted by fire twenty-four years ago, mother was killed in that blaze. Laura might have started the fire. She claims she doesn't remember what happened. For all our sakes, I wish I knew she was innocent. Mother and Laura never got along, always fighting..." Edward closed his eyes as though in pain.

"Laura told me about her mother's death. She was tormented by the thought that perhaps she'd killed her. But now Laura's dead, you've got to let it go."

"You're right. Antara is the one we need to help."

"She's in good hands with your Aunt Mary," Nelda assured him.

"I wonder," Edward said getting into the truck and slamming the truck door. "Be careful, Nelda."

She watched the truck drive away. Nelda had an uneasy feeling about him. Had he given her a veiled threat or did he think she was in danger?

As she turned off the porch light, she saw the headlights of another vehicle turn into the long winding drive. She stood up and waited near the door for their next visitor.

She recognized the sheriff's new, black truck and wondered why the late visit.

Joe Coates stepped out of his truck with an air of determination. "Good evening, Nelda, glad to see you've moved in all right."

He stepped up on the stone porch and Nelda could see his hair was neatly combed and his clothes could easily pass military inspection. She was impressed with his appearance, and especially with the smell of his Old Spice after shave lotion. Her favorite uncle had splashed it on after every shave and she loved the fragrance.

"Thanks, Joe. What brings you out so late?"

"Just making my evening rounds. Wanted to make sure you and your friend were okay. Was that Edward Finch leaving here as I drove up?"

Nelda tried to comb her hair by running her fingers through it, then gave up. Why did this man make her want to look her best?

"Yes it was. He came for some patio furniture Antara gave him. Would you like to come in and meet my friend, Sally?"

"I wish I had the time, but I haven't finished my rounds. How about the two of you joining me for lunch tomorrow at the Red Dragon restaurant in Smitherton? We need to talk."

Nelda was excited. He had some new information about the case he was going to share with her; she just knew it. She forgot about the way she looked and stepped closer to him and stumbled on an uneven stone. His strong hands reached out and grabbed her. For an electrifying minute he pulled her close, then quickly released her.

"How silly of me," Nelda said. "I guess it's time to pull off these shoes and go to bed. It's certainly been a busy day."

"I'm sorry I disturbed you so late, Nelda. Go on in and get some rest. Will I be seeing you tomorrow about twelve-thirty?"

"Of course. We'll be happy to have lunch with you. Thanks for being concerned about us."

He slowly walked back to his truck, climbed in and started the motor. Nelda stood in the cool night breeze and watched him drive away. There was definitely some attraction between them and she was beginning to enjoy it. Would this interfere with her ability to solve the case? Of course not. Her sleuthing instinct was too strong for romance to get in the way.

Slowly she walked back in the house and locked the door behind her. She was deep in thought when Sally, who had watched them from the window, bombarded her with questions.

"Who was that attractive man, Nelda? Don't tell me that's the sheriff you claim is giving you such a hard time." Sally sat down on the sofa and patted the cushion next to her. "Sit down and tell me all about him."

Nelda sighed and removed her shoes before settling on the couch next to Sally. She reached down and rubbed her feet. "Oh my aching feet, Sally. As much as I paid for these shoes from Jones' Sure Fit, my feet shouldn't be hurting."

"Let's not be coy, Nelda. I want the inside details of your friendship with this man."

"There's nothing much to tell. His name is Joe Coates and he's taken John's place as sheriff."

"You told me he was mean to you when all of you were questioned. He didn't look mean a few minutes ago." Sally's eyes twinkled as she looked at Nelda over her gold rimmed glasses.

"Well, let me explain about Joe. According to his secretary, he's not used to being around a strong-willed woman. His wife, who died several years ago, was sweet and meek. He did everything for her and he doesn't know what to make of me."

"A woman who can fend for herself, huh?"

"Yes, but I think there is a part of him that likes a woman who can solve her own problems."

"Sure, Nelda, he'd probably like to tame you."

"Ha! That's a good one. I'm afraid he wants to stop my meddling in his case."

"Still, there is something to be said about having a man to keep you company and warm your feet on a cold winter's night."

"Now listen to you. You haven't missed having a husband, and an electric blanket can do wonders for your feet."

Sally laughed. "So you're not going to have a romance?"

"I didn't say that, but not any time soon. Let's go to bed...I'm really beat."

"Suits me, but I wish you'd bring me up to date on all aspects of the case tomorrow."

"I promise."

Nelda went around checking all the outside doors before climbing the stairs. She supposed she or Sally could have stayed in Laura's big bedroom, but the thought of sleeping in her dead cousin's room made her shiver.

"Good night," she called to Sally as she walked down the hall to Laura's room."

"See you in the morning, Nelda," Sally responded.

The house was very quiet. Nelda couldn't even hear the A/C running. She wasn't used to such quietness. After dressing for bed, she stood on tiptoe in the middle of the mattress and removed the skate board poster from the ceiling. No smiling teenager was going to lull her to sleep, but if there was one of Robert Redford…

*   *   *

A small scraping noise woke Nelda from a troubled sleep. The dial of her travel clock glowed softly in the dark showing her it was 2:15 a.m. She wondered if Sally might be wandering around. Her old friend did have bouts with insomnia especially when sleeping in a strange bed.

Slipping on her robe, Nelda picked up her pencil flashlight and quietly opened the bedroom door leading to the hall. She looked toward Sally's room, but the door was closed. There was no sign of a light coming from anywhere. Once again, she heard a scraping noise. Listening intently, she realized it was coming from downstairs. When she reached Sally's room, Nelda opened the door. Her pencil sized beam of light showed Sally sound asleep. She closed the door gently and retreated to her own room. Now, the question was, should she proceed downstairs without a weapon of any kind? Was there anything at all that she could use to make the intruder go away? Searching Antara's closet, she found a skateboard propped up against the wall behind some winter clothes. It wasn't much of a weapon, but maybe the noise from it rolling would scare the intruder away.

Nelda's heart was doing overtime. How foolish of her not to unplug the kitchen phone and use it in the bedroom. Antara had taken her bedroom phone with her when she moved in with Mary.

With the heavy skateboard under her arm, Nelda made her way toward the stairs. There she stopped and listened. She groaned inwardly as a stair-step squeaked from someone's weight. The intruder moved slowly upward. Nelda decided it was time to take action. She set the skateboard down at the top of the stairs and pushed it with all her might. There was a scream as the skateboard made contact with the body below. The lights over the stairs suddenly came on, blinding Nelda. She lost her balance and rolled like a limp rag-doll down to the first landing. Sally, with her hand still on the light switch, looked down at Nelda with disbelief.

The sound of running footsteps and the banging of the backdoor could be heard as the intruder made his get away.

CHAPTER NINETEEN

Copycat

Poor Sally let out a little scream, then scrambled down the stairs to aid and comfort her fallen friend. Nelda lay there moaning with her eyes closed.

"Oh, Nelda, please tell me you're all right. Is anything broken? Please! oh please open your eyes."

"Just one minute," whispered Nelda. "As soon as my head quits swimming I'll open my eyes and check for broken bones." Nelda rubbed her right shoulder where it had hit the banister. A good thing it stopped her, or she would have rolled on down to the bottom of the stairs.

"I didn't realize you were standing near the stairs' edge when I turned on the lights. I'm going to call 911 and the sheriff." Sally turned to go back upstairs.

"No, Sally. Wait until I see how banged up I am." The last thing Nelda wanted to do was go to the hospital for observation. She didn't want that sheriff coming out in the middle of the night either.

Slowly Nelda opened her eyes. She could see, but her shoulder was throbbing like a teen's car amplifiers on a Saturday night. Slowly she stretched her right leg; there was hardly any pain. Next she tried her other limbs and nothing seemed broken. So good so far, but now it was time to get up.

"Praise the Lord, Sally, nothing is broken. I'm going to get up and go on downstairs."

"Why? You should come upstairs and see if you're truly all in one piece. Then, take something for your pain."

"All in good time. I've got to do something downstairs first." Sally reached out to help her, but Nelda struggled to her feet without her help.

"What about disturbing evidence down there, Nelda? Maybe the thief left fingerprints or some other clues."

"We're not disturbing anything. I'm going to see how the intruder got in the house. If it's through a door, we'll have to fix it so he can't come back in."

They made their way slowly down the stairs. Nelda rubbed her shoulder ever few feet wishing the pain would stop. When they reached the first floor, Sally turned on the overhead light in the living room. Nelda looked anxiously around the big room, but not one thing seemed to be out of place.

"Be sure not to handle anything down here, Sally."

"I'm not, but I don't think this room was disturbed."

"It looks that way," responded Nelda. "Now, let's check the kitchen and Laura's bedroom."

The kitchen showed no signs of disturbance, but Laura's bedroom looked as if a tornado had passed through it. All the drawers were emptied on the floor, and the bed was stripped down to the box springs. The clothes were out of the closets and the pockets were turned inside out. Even the pictures were pulled out of their frames. Someone did a through search, but Nelda doubted if they had found what they wanted. Why else would they be climbing the stairs?

Sally had a bewildered look and turned toward Nelda for a possible explanation. "Why would anyone destroy a room like this? It must be a madman."

"No, it looks like a professional search job," said Nelda. "To what end, I don't know. We stopped the thief from coming upstairs. I don't think he or she thought anyone was here."

"We did have our cars in the garage and all the lights out," said Sally. "Maybe it's just a case of theft and has nothing to do with Laura's death."

"Could be, but I still think they were looking for some particular thing."

They walked down the hall to the back door. Nelda tried the door and found it unlocked. "Sally, whoever it was has a key or has picked the lock. I know I locked both outside doors before we went to bed."

"He opened it somehow, Nelda. I heard the back door bang shut after you fell. You know we can't stay here now; it's not safe." Sally looked out the windows into the darkness.

"Nonsense, they won't come back tonight, but just in case they do we'll rig the front and back doors so they'll have a difficult time opening them."

Sally gave Nelda a doubtful look. "How are you going to do that?"

"We'll need two straight back chairs and some cooking pots."

After two trips to the kitchen, they were ready to barricade the outside doors. Nelda wedged the top rung of a chair under the door knob in the kitchen, then put two pots on the seat of the chair. "A little noise insurance," she said to Sally.

When they walked to the front door, they found a dead bolt securing it, and a large curved handle that was not conducive to the chair treatment.

"We're safe with this type of lock, Sally. Now let's go upstairs and try to get some sleep."

"What about the sheriff, Nelda. Shouldn't we call him tonight?"

"Absolutely not. If we get in bed now, we'll get a few hours sleep." She rubbed her shoulder, but the pain was subsiding. The fall was not as bad as she thought.

They trooped back upstairs and Nelda washed down a couple of aspirins. She laid her head on two feather pillows, but knew she wouldn't be able to go to sleep right away. Grabbing a pencil, she wrote out a list of things she needed to do the next day. Then she lay there with her eyes closed, and tried to make some sense of what had happened so far.

It all started with that trip to New Orleans, and the psychic telling her to *beware the color blue*. Not that she believed in fortune tellers, because she thought they were just out to make money. Was it coincidence that the color blue appeared at crucial moments?

At the family reunion, Laura said someone tampered with the brakes on her car. She thought it was her daughter. Then, at Antara's birthday party, Laura's drink is laced with strychnine. Laura died and now there are several suspects. One is Antara. It is really hard for Nelda to believe that Antara is guilty of trying to harm her mother. But she had to admit that Antara lied, at first, about her knowledge of cars. And of course, mother and daughter were always fighting.

Another suspect is the old man Dennis hired as a helper, Max Beaux. He holds a grudge against the Finch family dating back twenty-four years. Laura's father was the civil engineer that helped condemn part of the Beaux farm for a county road. There is no doubt that Max hates anyone that had anything to do with that project. He proved that by torching several homes built by people who had a hand in the roads' development.

What is Thomas Compton's involvement in the case? He certainly is a peculiar fellow, moody and obsessed with cleanliness, always washing his hands. She felt sure he was hiding something about his relationship with Laura. Could he be Antara's father? What caused Laura to break off her engagement with him?

The last suspect on the list is the one that would gain the most by Laura's death. Edward Finch inherited a sizable amount of money that would have gone to Laura on her fortieth birthday. He also argued with Laura about a loan just before her lemonade was poisoned. Just then Nelda found her thought processes going astray. Her mind refused to focus on the case any longer. It was floating away into never-never land. She'd have to fight the dragons when it was light.

* * *

Nelda woke with a start. She grimaced with pain as she tried to lift her head off the pillow. It wasn't only her shoulder that hurt, but her whole body ached. The sun was shining through the window and the clock showed 9:00 a.m. She made another try at sitting up and was successful this time. There was a knock at the door.

"Nelda, "Sally called while pushing the door open. "I bet I have something that will wake you up."

Nelda sat back against the pillows trying to smile while Sally presented a steaming cup of coffee to her on a small tray.

"Thank you, you wonderful friend," Nelda inhaled the aroma of black coffee and didn't complain that Sally forgot the cream.

"Did I hear you moaning in here?"

"You bet. I'm still not sure I'm going to live, but this coffee is sure going to help."

"You better get up and get dressed."

"Why?" Nelda took a sip of coffee before stretching out her legs.

"The sheriff is coming to see us and look at the damage the intruder made last night."

"How did he know about our night visitor? Did you call him?"

"Of course not. He called to make sure we'd meet him for lunch, and that's when I mentioned our night caller." Sally edged toward the door after seeing the frown on Nelda's face.

"Don't tell him about my fall," said Nelda. I don't want him looking me over for some sign of senility."

Nelda wished he'd come later. She wanted to take a long soak in a hot tub of water. She felt sure it would get rid of some of the aches and pains. She'd take a long soak anyway. The sheriff would just have to wait until she felt like talking to him.

Sally took the tray and cup downstairs as Nelda painfully made her way to the bathroom. As she drew a tub of water and removed her pajamas, she found, to her surprise, very few blue marks on her body. She credited her lack of bruises and broken bones to the exercise she received playing tennis.

Crawling into the tub of hot water was pure heaven. Nelda would have stayed longer than fifteen minutes, but realized she had to hurry if she wanted to get through the things on her list today.

First, she had to let Mary know about the break-in. She slipped on her robe and called Mary, who answered on the second ring.

"Hello, Mary, I wanted you to know that someone unlocked the back door last night and ransacked Laura's room."

"What! Oh Nelda, were you are Sally hurt?"

"No, we're both fine, but I'll have another lock put on the back door by tonight."

"It might be too dangerous for you to live there."

"No, it's going to be fine. The sheriff is coming to investigate. This afternoon Sally and I will put Laura's room in order."

"Be careful," begged Mary."

"I will. We'll call you later."

*   *   *

Nelda dressed in a cool grey dress, then brushed her hair while trying to avoid raising her arm very high. Her shoulder still hurt when she raised her right arm. As she added a touch of lipstick, Sally came up to tell her that the sheriff and another man from the department were there to look at Laura's room.

"I'm coming downstairs right now, Sally. And as soon as the sheriff leaves, let's head for the library. I want to see what the *Stearn Gazette* had to say about those fires that Max set so long ago."

"You mean we have to look through stacks of newspapers from back then?" Sally's face contorted with distaste.

Nelda laughed. "No, Sally, that would take forever. They have the newspapers on microfilm. We just go to the year we want and look for the arsons that occurred at that time."

"It still sounds like work, but I'm game."

Nelda thought Sally looked especially pretty. She had on a pink stripped cotton dress with white sandals. Her white hair was in natural curls around her head. What a wonderful gift naturally curly hair is, thought Nelda. She couldn't understand why some people hated their hair when it was that way.

"Hurry, Nelda, the sheriff is waiting to talk to you."

They walked downstairs to the waiting sheriff. His assistant was nowhere in sight. Nelda supposed he was dusting for fingerprints and looking for other evidence the intruder might have left behind.

"Good morning, Nelda, heard you had a little trouble last night." He didn't smile and his expression was deadly serious.

Nelda hesitated a few seconds before she answered. Joe was his spiffy self with hair neatly combed, face clean shaven, and a khaki uniform that looked new. Nelda knew if she got close enough, she'd smell his Old Spice after shave.

"Yes, as you've probably seen, someone got in last night and ransacked Laura's room. I rolled a skate board at the thief as he started up the stairs. Then he ran out the back door."

The sheriff listened and then shook his head. "Why didn't you call right away? I imagine there was a lot of noise when he was searching Laura's room."

"There was some noise, but no banging. I heard it because I'm a light sleeper. It seemed silly to disturb you at two in the morning. He was not coming back."

Joe's face and neck turned red and his hand clenched the pencil he was holding so tightly it broke in two pieces. In a controlled voice he said. "Would you mind calling me in a situation like this, so I could be the judge of whether I should come out right away?"

"Yes I'll do that. Is there any other way we can help you?" Nelda asked sweetly.

He unclenched his hands and looked down at the broken pencil. "No, my deputy and I will be dusting for fingerprints."

"Fine, we'll be in the kitchen having breakfast. After that we're leaving. I do have an extra key in case you're still here when we're ready to leave."

"May I give it back to you at lunch?" Joe asked Nelda.

"I'm really sorry, but can't have lunch with you today. Maybe another time." Nelda swept pass Joe on her way to the kitchen. She was right; he did smell like Old Spice.

*　*　*

"Why didn't you want to have lunch with Joe?" Sally asked Nelda as they entered the city library.

"Did you see how mad he was about me not calling him in the middle of the night?"

"Do you suppose this time he could have been right?"

"Maybe, but my judgment told me that once the culprit discovered there were people in the house, he wasn't coming back. At any rate, I wouldn't feel comfortable eating with a guy that just lost his temper with me."

"I guess so. But what a shame to turn down a free lunch."

Nelda laughed. "You old skinflint. If that's what's bothering you I'll pay for the meal."

"I suppose there is no way that I can help this romance get off the ground?"

"Afraid not, lets see if we can find the newspaper article about the Finch's fire. I remember when it happened, but twenty-four years is a long time."

Sally and Nelda entered the library and made their way around a group of small children led by a stern, portly woman. Definitely not the grandmotherly type thought Nelda, however if she's introducing them to books, hooray for her.

The microfilm machine was attached to a table that had drawers containing microfilm. Each stored roll of film contained a year of the *Stearn Gazette*. Nelda quickly selected the year she thought would cover the fire and started the search. Sally sat beside her. As they scrolled through the pages of the local paper, there were many news items that intrigued them, because they knew the people mentioned in the articles. Just when they thought they would never find it, bingo.

"Oh, Nelda, they even show the man suspected of burning the house."

"Yes," Nelda seemed startled. "It's a young-looking Max Beaux."

"How did he answer the accusation? I can't quite make out his statement."

"He said what he's always contended, *It's a damn copycat. I torched the rest, but I shore didn't burn the Finch house.*" Nelda's frustration was beginning to build. Why would he admit to the others and not this one?

CHAPTER TWENTY

Life In A Dish

The doorbell woke Nelda from a sound sleep at 8:15 a.m. Could she have slept that late? For shame, the best part of the day would be over before she even got going. She and Sally had stayed up until the wee hours straightening up Laura's room and visiting.

Nelda grabbed her robe, slipped it on and walked downstairs. She peeked out the blinds and found the locksmith standing on the front porch with a tool box. It was Don Barnes dressed in blue overalls. His unruly white hair was falling in his face almost covering up his faded blue eyes. Nelda wondered where he'd found a pair of overalls big enough to go over his stomach. She worried about his overweight, because diabetes ran in his family.

After unlocking the door, she pulled it open. "Don, nice of you to come out so soon. I guess I haven't seen you since you replaced the locks on my house last year."

"I expect so. Sorry about the fire at your place. I hope you can go home soon."

"Thank you. Things will work out."

"After you called, Mary Finch phoned me. She wanted to make sure I put on some good locks."

"I appreciate that," said Nelda. "Guess you better check in the real estate lockbox and see if the key is missing. Mary said that key locked both the front and back doors."

"I'll do that. I'm going to put a night lock on the back door. The front door already has one."

"Fine," Nelda turned to go.

"Are you having some trouble out here, Nelda?"

"Break-in night before last, but I don't think they got anything."

"Well, I just saw the sheriff coming out from your road. Guess he was making sure they didn't come back last night."

All at once, Nelda felt guilty. Joe was looking out for them. Maybe she shouldn't have been so hard on him. Still, his temper wasn't a good sign. There was too much going on; Nelda's mind was in a muddle. What she needed was to get away for a while. Maybe a little trip with Sally would ease the tension.

She hadn't set the automatic timer on the coffee pot last night, so Nelda made straight for the kitchen and found that Sally had already made the coffee. Nelda shook her head; this sleeping 'till eight had to stop. Depression set in, because she missed her home and daily routine. Was she ever going to play tennis again? Her muscles ached from lack of exercise.

Looking around the unfamiliar kitchen, Nelda spotted a small TV. Great! She could get the 8:30 news. Turning it on, Nelda found the local channel Four with Evelyn Chasing, the roving reporter. She was interviewing Carl Hanks, Joe's young deputy, in front of the sheriff's office. They stood under a big oak tree. Evelyn's blonde hair had changed from last year to a much longer hair style. The new hairdo was very becoming, thought Nelda. She turned up the volume, and sat on a kitchen stool with a cup of coffee.

"Now, Mr. Hanks, could you tell us about the break-in at the old Finch place?"

Carl Hanks was enjoying his debut on television. Instead of looking at Evelyn when he answered, he looked directly at the camera with a silly smile on his face. His boyish thin face and slicked down brown hair gave him the appearance of Barney Fife on the Andy Griffith Show.

"Nothing to tell." He said. "I guess somebody thought there wasn't nobody there, so they just decided to go in and see what they could steal. Miss Finch's bedroom was a mess. I don't think they had a chance to steal anything." He put his lower lip out and shook his head from side to side.

Evelyn pushed back her hair. "Is this the home where Laura Finch was poisoned.?"

"Yes, but I'm sure the two incidents didn't have anything in common."

The station showed some footage of the log house on that fateful day, and Nelda cringed from the painful memories.

"Well, Deputy, has Sheriff Coates had any breaks in this murder?"

"We're going to make an arrest any day now," Carl answered in a smug tone.

Nelda almost fell off the stool. She should have had lunch with Joe. Maybe this was what he was going to tell her.

"Really," said the vivacious blonde, holding her flaring blue skirt down with one hand and clutching the mike with the other. The wind caused her hair to whip across her face, temporarily blinding her. The interview ended then with Evelyn promising her TV audience additional information about the upcoming arrest.

Nelda turned the set off and practically ran up the stairs. "Sally," she called, "we've got to get going. You know we have an appointment to visit Thomas today."

"What's wrong, Nelda? You sound upset."

"It's that silly deputy, Carl Hanks. He said on TV that the sheriff will soon make an arrest in Laura's death."

"Do you suppose that's true?" Sally asked, while buckling her sandals.

"I doubt it. Joe is all hung up on arresting Max, but I don't believe he was the one who poisoned Laura. It's not his style. Look, our appointment with Thomas is at 10:00 a.m. I'll get dressed and we'll go over to his clinic for a tour. Then, I want you and I to plan a trip. What do you say?"

"Suits me. Why are you standing there looking out the window?"

"I was just thinking. Suppose Laura's father made another will before he died, naming Laura and Antara as his heirs, and Edward thinks his father hid the will somewhere in this house. That might explain why the old pictures of his parents were stripped from their frames."

"That's pretty ridiculous, Nelda. Why wouldn't he look for the will right after his father died?"

"He didn't need to then. In the will that was found, his father gave him half the estate, but he squandered it all. If another will were produced with Antara as the heir, he'd be penniless."

"Edward knew we were here. He wouldn't try to raid the house with us in it, would he?"

"I guess it depends on how desperate he is." Nelda twisted on the ruby ring Sue had given her. It was a sure sign of nervous fatigue.

* * *

Nelda couldn't care less about the workings of a fertility clinic, but she knew that to understand the relationship between Laura and Thomas it was important to visit the clinic and learn as much as she could.

It was 9:50 a.m. when Nelda and Sally drove up in front of Thomas' clinic in Smitherton. They were both surprised to see the architecture of the building. It didn't look like a clinic, but an old plantation brick home. There was a large, wooden front porch, white columns and six long windows with green shutters. The porch was picture perfect with hanging baskets of Boston fern, and comfortable looking wooden chairs spaced several feet apart. White ceiling fans moved slowly with the warm breeze.

"I know this is an old Smitherton home transformed into a clinic," Nelda said. "I'll be anxious to see how the inside of the house was treated."

"Me too," said Sally smoothing out her white cotton dress.

It was just a little cooler today, but both women had dressed to accommodate the over 90 degree weather. Nelda wore a short flowered skirt with matching blouse and white sandals. The sleeves of her blouse were long enough to cover the bruise on her arm caused by the fall.

As they approached the front steps, Nelda noticed the addition of a porch ramp to accommodate wheelchair patients. She thought that strange for such a clinic, but then realized that the physically handicapped should have the opportunity to be parents too.

The door swung open easily and they found themselves in the original parlor of the house. It was furnished with antiques. Even the chandeliers looked as if they might be the original ones. A buzzer sounded. It was no doubt activated by their presence in the room. She and Sally looked toward a door that opened to a room beyond and waited for someone to appear. Thomas came rushing out to greet them.

"Good morning, Ladies, you are right on time." He grabbed Nelda by the hand.

"Thank you for inviting us, Thomas," replied Nelda. "We're looking forward to the tour." She noticed that his hand was moist, as if he had just washed his hands, and didn't have time to dry them properly.

"We were certainly surprised that you decided to have your clinic in this beautiful old house," Sally said. She looked around the room with a smile of genuine appreciation for all the antique furniture.

"Thank you. My clinic started downtown, but the space was too small, so we ended up here. This was the Sharp's ancestral home. When they sold it furnished, the new owners converted it into a bed and breakfast, but it didn't work out for them. That's when I bought it."

"I suppose the rest of the house is completely remodeled?" Nelda asked.

"I'm afraid so. We completely gutted the rest of the home to build a couple of labs, examination rooms and office. Even the back-porch was enclosed for one of the labs. Laura bought several pieces of antique furniture from me for her home. But I'm sure you'll be glad to know we do have a small kitchen upstairs that has fresh coffee."

Thomas led them into a long hall with a glassed-in lab on the left. There were two examination rooms on the right, and a comfortable looking office with a library at the end of the hall, next to the stairway.

He chatted with them as they climbed the stairs. "I live up here," he explained. "When I bought this place, I couldn't afford a place of my own. Now I can, but see no need to move. All the employees use the kitchen and dining area at meal time. That way they cannot be late from their lunch hour." He laughed, but only with his mouth. His eyes showed no mirth.

From the landing, they entered a small modern kitchen. "Sit here at the bar." Thomas pointed to some tall stools with backs on them. The coffee had a familiar aroma. It also smelled fresh and strong.

"It's StarBucks House Blend isn't it, Thomas?"

"Good olfactory nerves, Nelda. It was Laura's favorite."

He poured coffee into mugs and placed the steaming cups in front of them, as they sat on the stools. Sally and Nelda doctored their coffee with sugar and coffee cream. Then Nelda savored the flavor before she spoke.

"You're right about Laura and her coffee," said Nelda. "When she and I were out together in New Orleans, this is the coffee she ordered, but they didn't have it, only dark roast Community."

"Oh, did she talk about me when you were together?" There was real sorrow in his eyes. Nelda looked at his slender tapered hands and decided he had a sensitive nature. She didn't know what his hands had to do with her decision, but it did.

"All she told me was that she didn't approve of some of the techniques you used in the lab. She didn't tell me what she objected to. Can you tell me what she was talking about.?"

Thomas glanced at Sally. Sally spoke up quickly. "Would you rather I leave?"

"I see no reason for that, Sally. I can assure Thomas that this information will be in confidence."

"I have broken no laws, and the sheriff knows this information, but I will share it with you too, Nelda."

"There are several reasons men and women come to our clinic. Sometimes they want their eggs or sperm stored for later use because they are not ready to have a child. Then, there are those that are having trouble conceiving. The man might have too few sperm or the woman has trouble ovulating. This is when we can step in and help."

"How do you do that?" Nelda asked.

"If the woman can no longer ovulate. We find a suitable donor who is willing to give up her eggs."

"Is that what Laura objected to?"

"Yes, that and the large doses of hormones we gave the donor, so that she would produce several eggs. Laura believed over a period of time it would harm the donor, but the doctors who work with me don't think so."

"That's it? That was her reason for breaking off your engagement and quitting the clinic?" Nelda had a gut feeling that this explanation was all wrong. Surely Laura had some other reason. Thomas was not leveling with her. Laura had worked at the clinic for many years. If this was the reason, she'd have quit years ago.

"That was the reason she gave. For the last several years, Laura was under a lot of stress."

"Do you know why?" Nelda asked, finishing her coffee.

"Antara was one reason. Did you know Laura was going to send her to a boarding school?"

"No, but I'm not surprised. Was there any other reason for her stress?"

"Edward borrowed a great deal of money from her."

Nelda shook her head. Why was Thomas being so candid with her? Was he trying to give Antara and Edward a reason for murder? She vowed to find out more about this man who was obsessed with cleanliness.

"Well let's start the tour," said Sally.

The lights were on in the second laboratory at the end of the hall. Nelda could see an Oriental man working at a stainless steel sink. She waited patiently for Thomas at the entrance to the laboratory.

"No, Nelda, this laboratory is off-limits to visitors. It's for commercial projects. We will tour the other one."

This statement made Nelda very curious. She turned and stared through the glass partition. She couldn't help noticing a set of blue files on a desk in the corner. The strangest feeling came over her. *Nelda Sees Blue.*

Touring the second lab was just a walk-through. Sally and Nelda looked at the microscopes, distillation equipment, racks of test tubes, vacuum hood and other equipment arrayed on immaculate laboratory tables, but Thomas gave no explanation of their use. He did mention that some of the babies started their lives in petri dishes.

When they arrived at the office and library, Nelda scrutinized the book shelves. There were two books that fascinated her, one was about cloning and the other was devoted to the use of stem cells.

"Thomas, are you interested in cloning or using stem cells for experimentation?" Nelda asked.

"No, I wouldn't think of it. It is immoral for you to suggest that."

You protest too much, thought Nelda. She was now even more curious about what was happening in the lab that was off-limits.

CHAPTER TWENTY-ONE

Swing Low Sweet Chariot

Nelda, Sally, and Mary stood around the dining room table in Laura's great room wrapping figurines in tissue paper. The large china cabinet that had contained them was now bare and surrounded by packing boxes.

"I'm really happy you're helping me pack these away," said Mary. "I certainly wouldn't want the next person who broke in here to walk off with these valuable pieces."

The collection consisted of Hummels, Royal Doultons, and Raimonds. Sally glanced under a Hummel figurine and did a double take when she saw how much it was worth. "My word, this boy and girl sitting on a fence with lambs nearby is now worth four-hundred dollars. Where ever did Laura find these?"

"They were Laura's mother's collection bought many years ago," Nelda said. "Laura had them priced and placed the sticker underneath them. Many of these figurines are discontinued." She admired a Royal Doulton piece of an old lady nodding off. It was labeled "Forty Winks" and priced now at three-hundred and twenty-five dollars.

"My goodness," said Mary. "If the burglar had known how much he could get for these collections, he wouldn't have torn up Laura's room."

"I'm not so sure, Mary," Nelda said. "Whoever did that was looking for a document or papers of some kind. Why else would they strip the bed and rip the pictures out of their frames?"

"It could be," said Mary. She then turned her attention to Sally. "Now, Sally, tell me about the trip you and Nelda are making to Houston."

Sally stretched her legs and arms and plopped down on the sofa. "Well, it's Nelda who has all the rich relatives. Sue phoned Nelda's cousin, Carolyn Crane, in Houston and told her we were coming to big H, and Carolyn insisted that we stay with her. She and her husband, Charles, own a huge house right on the golf course. They've even planned an outing for us."

"But you're not going unless you get up, and help us finish this packing," Nelda said, but her smiling brown eyes betrayed her bluff.

Grumbling, Sally muttered "slave driver" and got up to help. They were wrapping their last few pieces when there was a knock on the door. Nelda peeked out the blind and saw the familiar pickup in the driveway.

"That's the sheriff out there. I wonder why he's here," Nelda said.

Mary spoke up. "I told him you were leaving for Houston tomorrow, and we needed extra patrolling out here. Maybe he's come to ask about that."

Nelda's heart gave a little flutter. She slipped her shoes back on and walked to the door to let him in. Why was it that every time he came around she looked a mess, lipstick all gone, and hair as limp as the spaghetti they'd had for lunch?

She pulled the door open. His blue eyes were smiling at her from under a new straw hat. Nelda couldn't help smiling back. "Good afternoon, Joe. Would you like to come in?"

"Thanks, Nelda," he said after removing his hat. "I hope this is not a bad time. I saw Ms. Finch's car in the drive and wanted to put her mind at ease about someone patrolling this area while you're in Houston."

Nelda stepped aside while Joe made his entry. Mary acted delighted to see the lawman. Even Sally perked up and smiled at Nelda, who tried not to meet her glance.

"Joe is here to assure you someone will be looking after the place, Mary."

"Thank you, Sheriff," said Mary. "That sure makes me feel better."

"Well, we'll do our best. I've visited all the neighbors and they'll keep an eye open for strangers in the day time. Then at night we'll come by as often as we can."

Nelda motioned for Joe to sit down. "Afraid I can't stay, but I would like a word with you on the porch if you don't mind."

"Okay. I guess they can do without me for a while."

Joe followed Nelda and closed the door. Moving away from the windows, she sat down in the swing at the end of the porch. Joe pulled up a rocking chair and brushed the dust out of it with his hat. He then sat down holding the hat in his big hands.

"Are you going to be away long?"

"No, just two or three days sightseeing and shopping. We've also been invited to the Glenn Miller Orchestra concert."

Joe smiled. "I could have sworn he died in the forties."

Of course she knew he was teasing, but played along. "Wrong! He'll be there with Elvis as his guest."

Both had a good laugh and then grew silent. Shadows appeared as the late evening sun slipped behind a cloud. Nelda looked up in the sky as a red tailed hawk soared by. She and Joe watched as it scoured the nearby woods before disappearing.

"Are you going to visit Laura's friend, Yvonne Sands, while you're there?" His eyes had a troubled look as he waited for her answer.

"Yes. I believe the only way to find the murderer is to understand Laura's past."

"I'm afraid for you, Nelda. What will the murderer do next?"

"I don't know. Have you ruled out Max as the killer?"

"I haven't ruled out anybody. Antara, Max, Thomas and Edward all had motives. We just don't have the evidence to make an arrest."

"If I get a chance to talk to Yvonne, I'll let you know. Have you talked with her?"

"Yes, but Yvonne said she couldn't help me, because she doesn't know anything."

Nelda got out of the swing. "I'll be okay," she said smiling. "It will be good to get away."

Joe stood too. He grasped Nelda's hand and squeezed it. "Don't forget about that dinner I owe you. You need to collect it soon."

"I will, as soon as we get back." Nelda walked to the door as Joe waved good-bye with his hat and climbed into his truck. She brushed a mosquito off her arm as she opened the door and hurried inside.

"What was that all about," asked Sally when Nelda closed the door.

"Oh nothing. He just wanted to know when we were coming back. I think he still wants to take us to dinner."

"You to dinner," Sally said. "When we return I'm going home to see about Sugar. I know that old dog is missing me."

Mary rubbed her shoulders and stretched. "Well girls, I've got to go home and take care of Antara. Thanks for helping me pack these things. I'll have someone pick them up tomorrow. You two have fun and promise to forget about Laura's death for a while."

"Not making any promises I can't keep," Nelda said. "But we'll be careful."

After Mary left, they went upstairs to pack and make phone calls. Nelda's house would be more vulnerable with her gone. She wanted to make sure her neighbors and Sue guarded it well.

* * *

Nelda woke up early wondering what to do with her antique comic book collection. She now had them stored in the bedroom closet. If something happened to them, she'd never get over it. She'd been collecting them all her life. Occasionally, she even opened up the box they were stored in and read one, especially the Superman series. It took her back to her childhood.

From her prone position on the bed, she stared up at the ceiling. It was then she discovered a ceiling tile that was not quite right. It looked as if someone had taken it out and replaced it, leaving a space between it and the adjacent tiles. She hadn't noticed it when she removed the poster from the ceiling. Why, thought Nelda, would anyone remove a ceiling tile and put it back? To hide something that's what.

She almost fell off the bed in her eagerness to explore what might be in the space overhead. Nelda could hardly reach the ceiling, so she got her old Samsonite suitcase out of the closet and stepped on it to remove the tile. Reaching into the opening, she drew out a handful of insulation. Stuffing that back in, she tried again and was rewarded this time when she found a journal of some kind. Withdrawing the book from the space, she let herself fall back on the bed with a thud.

"Nelda!" Sally cried, as she rushed into the room. "Are you all right? I heard this terrible sound as though you fell out of bed."

"In bed, that's how I fell. Look at what I found in the ceiling." She lifted the journal high and grinned at Sally.

"Well, I hope it was worth taking a chance on a broken bone." Sally tied the belt on her cotton robe with a jerk. She adjusted her glasses on the end of her nose and plopped down beside Nelda. "Who does that journal belong to? Antara?"

"I don't know," said Nelda adjusting her gown. "Hand me my glasses on the bedside table and we'll find out."

Nelda opened up the journal and gave a little cry. "Someone has torn most of the pages out."

"Did you find out who it belonged to?" Sally moved closer to Nelda.

"I believe it's Laura's. These two pages tell about her car accident."

"Well what does she say? Does she know who was responsible?"

"No, and the other pages just describe her New Orleans trip. Everything else is torn out."

"It was Antara who ripped the pages out, wasn't it, Nelda?"

"I don't know. I had convinced myself that Antara had nothing to do with her mother's death." Tears formed in Nelda's eyes.

"It's all right, Nelda. I'm sure Antara is not guilty of killing her mother. Let's just put this aside for now and get on our way."

"Right, let's do it. I'll just store my comic books at Mary's house on the way out. I don't trust anything in this house to be safe." Nelda decided she'd add Laura's picture album from the coffee table to her box of books, just as a precaution. Somehow the album haunted her, as if there might be a solution to Laura's murder in it.

*   *   *

Their drive to the suburban area of Houston was pleasant, but not as colorful as in spring or fall. Green trees and wilted vegetation dotted the landscape even though some leaves had tinges of red or yellow. As they approached Carolyn's subdivision, they drove past a pasture filled with Arabian horses. A large barn with stalls was built at the back of the property. Only the rich, thought Nelda, could afford to keep a horse for a pet in the city.

113

"Look for the country church, Sally. That's where we turn into Lost Pines, Carolyn's subdivision."

They drove a mile or so until Sally sang out. "There is the entrance and it is fancy. Can't wait to see their home."

*   *   *

The Crane's residence was huge, at least six or seven thousand square feet, as were all the homes in the area. Carolyn's was made of limestone from the Texas hill country and situated on a cul-de-sac with their backyard adjoining the golf course. The sixth tee was practically in their swimming pool.

Nelda and Sally approached the double front doors with excitement. What fun it was to get away for a while, and have someone plan their entertainment. The door opened before Nelda could push the door bell; Carolyn was standing there to welcome them. The buxom blonde woman wore a loose fitting, green chiffon dress. She drew them into the foyer with a smile and hug. Her husband, Charles, was right behind her with a shy smile and a hand shake.

"Great timing, you two, Charles is treating us to dinner before the concert. You have time for a quick tour of the house before we leave."

Charles waved good-bye to them as he retreated to the patio. In contrast to Carolyn, he was tall and thin with graying hair, and had an air of detachment about him. Nelda didn't mind, because she knew Carolyn would keep them busy.

"Well let's start here," Carolyn said. "The dining room is to your right and the wine room is located just beyond. There are three living areas, four bedrooms, five bathrooms, and two offices. A balcony overlooking the golf course and swimming pool is on the second floor, and there are wonderful views from every room."

Nelda was happy for her cousin's success. She had struggled many years with ailing parents and wayward children and deserved some happiness.

They wandered through the beautiful home trying to take it all in. Each room was tastefully decorated and immaculate. Nelda wondered how much time it would take her to clean such a house. She greatly admired the home, but was thankful for her old house even if the water did rumble in the pipes.

Forty minutes later they joined Charles on the patio. He continued watching the greens even as they drew near, not saying a word. Certainly a strange way to act, thought Nelda.

"Edward, where are your manners?" Carolyn said in a loud voice.

"Be quiet, Carolyn. Some man is watching the house from the golf course. He's been doing that every since I got out here."

Nelda anxiously turned her eyes toward the greens and tried to locate the person Ed was talking about. Was it possible someone had followed them? Whoever killed Laura could be mentally unstable and after her too. But why? She didn't know anything, but the killer didn't know that. And just maybe the killer was afraid of what she could find out from Yvonne. Nelda tried not to show her concern for Sally's sake.

"I don't see anyone except the two men putting on the sixth green. Is he one of them?" Carolyn asked.

"No, he was Oriental and has disappeared now, but let's be sure to turn the security system on when we leave. And that should be about now."

* * *

Charles had made their dinner reservations at a new steak house right across the street from where the concert was to take place. It was a pleasure not to wait in line.

After they were seated, Nelda studied the wine menu while a white-jacketed waiter stood by to take her order. She was flustered by the long list of wines. Charles came to her rescue.

"Nelda, could I suggest a wine I know you and Sally will love?"

"Yes indeed. I'm afraid I'm no connoisseur of good wines."

"Waiter," Charles said, "we'll have a bottle of 1997 Sonoma County Chardonnay."

After receiving her wine, Nelda sipped on it appreciatively enjoying the fruity flavors. She promised herself to learn how to choose from a wine list, not that she would have much use for that knowledge.

By the time their steak orders arrived, they were wondering if they would make it to the concert on time. They finished their meal in haste. What a shame, thought Nelda, to rush through such a lovely meal.

As they left the restaurant, Charles spoke to Carolyn in a hushed voice. "There is the guy that was watching our house from the golf course."

"Are you sure?" Carolyn asked.

"No," laughed Charles. "You know all those Orientals look alike to me.

Nelda did not laugh. Thomas had a Chinese lab assistant. Could it be him? Of course not, she reasoned. They were a hundred miles from home.

Sally looked over at Nelda, who just shrugged and gave no sign she was disturbed by the incident. Nelda decided that there was no point in ruining everyone's evening with her suspicions that were probably unfounded.

$$* \quad * \quad *$$

Nothing spoiled their evening. Nelda and Sally were still reliving the concert the next morning while dressing for breakfast.

"Wasn't that music fabulous, Nelda? It was amazing how many pieces of Glenn Miller's music I remembered, *Sunrise Serenade, Little Brown Jug,* and *Don't sit under the Apple Tree,* to name a few. It really took me back," Sally said dreamily, brushing her hair.

"Me too," said Nelda, slipping on her skirt. "And I'm so glad they played my favorite, *Stardust.* Jim and I danced many times to that one."

"Have you tried calling Yvonne yet?" Sally asked.

"I did, last night, but her roommate said she was out. I left a message for her to call me back this morning. I'll try again before we go to the museum."

After dressing, Nelda and Sally went downstairs to breakfast. The dinette table was located in an open area that included the kitchen and family room. It looked out over the swimming pool and golf course, a really wonderful view.

Carolyn was sitting there with a concerned look on her face. "Nelda, Yvonne Sands' roommate just called. It seems Yvonne didn't come home last night. She reported her missing."

Nelda held her breath. All she could think of was that beautiful, talented girl could be in mortal danger or already dead. The killer knew that Yvonne had been Laura's closest confidante. For some reason a line from a spiritual she'd heard at the concert popped into her head, Swing low sweet chariot, coming for to carry me home.

CHAPTER TWENTY-TWO

Visit to the Shrink

Nelda and Sally spent three days in Houston hoping that some clue to Yvonne's whereabouts would surface. It didn't. They knew there was nothing they could do to help, so reluctantly they packed their bags and left for Stearn.

The road seemed a lot longer to Nelda going back. "I feel so guilty, Sally. I know our visit had something to do with Yvonne's disappearance."

"Well maybe it happened sooner by your visit, but Yvonne must have some knowledge the murderer wishes she didn't have."

"If I only knew what. I just pray she's not dead." Nelda wiped her eyes with the back of her hand.

"Let's not talk about it anymore. It will be good to get back home to Sugar. He'll be so happy to see me."

"I'm sure that's true." Nelda had to smile, because Sally treated her dog like a child. Sometimes, Nelda thought about getting a dog. She'd always had one, but when they died it was all too painful. Besides, what a nuisance they were when you want to go somewhere.

"What are you going to do next?" Sally asked as she adjusted her seat belt.

"Get back in my own house and have a sane life again. My plants are probably all dead and I haven't had any exercise in so long my legs hurt at night."

"Let's not forget the romance with the sheriff." Sally cut her eyes over to Nelda.

"You're making an orchestra out of a violin. Nothing has happened and I'm not sure I want it to." Nelda slowed down and stopped for a school bus. They were almost home.

"You can't fool me about getting off the case, Nelda. You probably have your next step all set up."

"Yes I do, and I'll tell you about it before you leave. But now, let's swing around to my house, before going to Laura's. I want to see how close Sam Godfrey is to finishing his repair work. I can't wait to get back in my own home."

Nelda's car moved toward her old street like a homing pigeon. She had forgotten how pretty her street was with all the big, mature trees. Even though the street was breaking up in places, she knew where to dodge the pot holes.

"There it is, Sally, gleaming in the evening sun. I don't see any black stuff on the siding, and luck is with me. There's Sam's truck; he'll be able to tell me when I can move back home."

She pulled up in the driveway and got out of the station wagon. The first things Nelda noticed were her plants; they all looked good, except for the ones destroyed by the firemen. Her frame of mind improved appreciably. Frank, her neighbor's kid, was doing a really good job of watering. She'd remember that when she paid him on Saturday.

Sam saw Nelda get out and rushed over to her. "Ms. Simmons, I've got some good news. I'm through with the inside, and you can move back in, but it will take me a few more days on the outside walls."

Nelda felt like hugging his neck, but immediately the desire vanished when she saw tobacco juice in the corner of his mouth. "That's just wonderful. I can't wait to be back home, and put everything in place. I'll be back with my bags tomorrow."

Sam was beaming as he waved good-bye to Nelda and Sally. "See there, Sally, City people don't know what they're missing by not knowing all the tradesmen. It's like having good friends working for you."

"That's true and you know which ones to avoid too."

Twenty minutes later they were driving up Laura's long drive. Several cars were parked in front of the house. One of the cars belonged to the real estate agency that had Laura's house listed. Nelda wondered what was happening.

Cindy Cassin, Brazos Realty agent, saw Nelda and hurried to the car.

"Great news, Nelda. I just had some folks sign an earnest money contract on this land. Soon we won't have to worry about fire insurance anymore." Her round face wore a big smile. It reminded Nelda of the popular yellow sticker with a smiley face.

"Wonderful," she replied. "Makes me feel better about clearing out tomorrow. Did you say land?"

"Yes, they don't want the house. They're going to tear it down, and build a modern one."

It saddened Nelda to see all the new people moving into the community. Pretty soon their small town would stretch all the way to Houston. She shuddered at the thought.

"I suppose it would take a fortune to make the log house into a modern home, but I hate to see it go. I don't suppose Antara had any choice."

"I think she and Ms. Finch were happy to get it off the market."

"What about the furniture?"

"I understand there is to be an estate auction."

"I see," said Nelda with a grim face. She couldn't mask the displeasure she felt for Edward and Antara's attitude toward the family antiques. Sure, some of the furniture had been purchased recently, but several of the pieces had been in the Finch family for many generations. They had even survived the fire set in the house twenty-four years ago.

"Well, we'll be getting out of your way now. Have a good night, Nelda."

Nelda went back to the car and waited for the realty people and prospective new owners to clear the driveway. While sitting there, she briefed Sally on what Cindy had told her about the status of the house and land.

"I wish I had room for some of those antiques, but my old house is stuffed to the gills," Sally said.

"Mine too. Some day Antara will be sorry she didn't keep a few of them. I really didn't appreciate antiques until I was almost forty."

"And that was only yesterday," Sally said as she and Nelda pulled into the garage.

Laughing, they unloaded their luggage and trooped into the house. Nelda had so much to do that her mind was already making out a list for tomorrow.

* * *

Over breakfast Nelda told Sally her immediate plans. "You see, Sally, the murderer has to be someone that was at the birthday party. The problem is to find out who had the strongest motive for seeing Laura dead. The next person I'll turn to for answers is Dr. Shirley Long, the psychologist Laura visited."

"You don't think Joe has already talked with her?"

"Probably, but I want to hear what she's got to say, too. Laura's life was very complex, with so many people giving her a hard time. Which one found it necessary to kill her?"

"Good question," responded Sally. It could have been her daughter, brother, lover or the grungy, old grudge holder. That's why you have to be careful. The closer you get to the truth, the more danger you're in."

"I know. Finish your oatmeal and I'll help you load up." Nelda was still dressed in her robe and slippers. She intended to leave right after Sally left. Her own bed would sure feel good tonight.

They both got busy washing up in the kitchen. Nelda didn't envy Mary with her job of moving things out of the house. There were hundreds of little items. Laura's drawers and cabinets were filled with trinkets she'd pick up from God knows where. Trying to price them would certainly be a problem. However, she'd see if she could help with the sale. But first things first, it was back home and a trip to see Dr. Long, if the doctor would talk to her.

* * *

Nelda waved good-bye to Sally with a promise to keep her informed if any break in the case occurred. She then checked all the windows and doors to make sure they were locked, loaded her luggage and breathed a sigh of relief as she headed for home. When she got home she called Dr. Long's office. Nelda was forced to leave a message on the doctor's answering system. All those machines in modern day communication made Nelda's blood pressure rise. "*Sa la vie,*" muttered Nelda as she turned her attention to getting her kitchen in order. She was busy displaying her milk glass behind the glass doors of her freshly painted cabinets when the phone rang. It was the sheriff.

"Nelda, welcome home. Sue called and said you were back. The police in Houston called me about Yvonne Sands disappearance. They still don't know what happened to her."

"How did they find out you knew her?"

"Several days ago I called one of the detectives I know, and talked to him about the case. There was an unofficial watch on her apartment."

"Didn't do any good," said Nelda mournfully.

"She may have left of her own accord."

"Maybe, but frightened to death, and without any luggage." Nelda's voice shook.

"Could I pick you and your friend up for dinner tonight, Nelda? We have plenty to talk about."

"Okay, but Sally has gone home now. We won't have a chaperone."

"Too bad," he said, laughing. "I'll see you at seven."

Nelda was thinking about calling Long's office again when her phone rang. It was the doctor.

"Ms. Simmons, this is Shirley Long returning your call. What can I do for you?"

Nelda didn't know exactly how to approach the doctor for information about Laura's death. She quickly decided that the best approach was a candid one. Just lay it all out for her. If it didn't fly, at least she'd have no regrets about trying.

"I'm Laura Finch's cousin. Her daughter, Antara, said you were her doctor, and I wanted to talk to you about Laura's death."

"I've heard of you and your detective work. I don't think I'll be able to help you. I've told the sheriff all I know."

"Would you at least spare me a few minutes? I promise not to make a pest of myself."

"Could you be at my office in one hour?"

"Yes, and thank you for returning my call."

She put the phone down, pushed back her hair, and gave a sigh of relief. She wondered how much the doctor would tell her about her talks with Laura. Because her patient was murdered, it would surely make a difference in how much information she'd divulge. Would the doctor tell a relative more than she had the sheriff? Nelda held out some hope.

What should she wear to visit a psychologist? Nelda decided something simple, but sort of dressy. When she opened up her closet door and peered inside, a slight smoky odor emanated from the hanging contents. Nelda could have cried. She removed a navy blue cotton dress from its hanger, hurried to the utility room, sprayed it with clothes fresh and put it in the dryer. While the dress was spinning, she went to the bathroom, applied makeup and combed her hair. When she went back, she pulled the dress out and smiled, odor all gone. Maybe some of these new fantastical products weren't so bad after all. Ten minutes later she was ready to visit the doctor.

* * *

Shirley Long's office was in an old building in the center of town, parking was not a problem. There were plenty of parking spaces on Main Street. The main shopping centers had left downtown Stearn. Now the new stores were located on the bypass. Nelda fretted about this trend all the time, because downtown stores suffered. Several attempts had been made to rejuvenate the inner city, but the public refused to shop there. She noticed most of the spaces were taken up with antique shops, second hand book stores, Mom & Pop restaurants and lawyers' offices. Nelda supposed the rent was considerably lower here than in the newer strips.

Dr. Long's office had been remodeled. The building still smelled old inside, however an attempt had been made to modernize it with recessed lighting and the ultracontemporary design of the vinyl floor. Nelda stopped in front of a frosted glass door with the doctor's name on it. Should she knock or just go on in? Her problem was solved when Thomas Compton opened the door, and rushed by her without a hint of recognition. His head was bowed and he was drying his hands on a handkerchief. Standing in the open doorway was a smallish woman in a green suit that Nelda supposed was the doctor. She had a strong face with deep set eyes, high cheek bones and sharp chin.

"Are you Nelda Simmons?" The woman asked. "I'm Dr. Shirley Long."

"Yes," said Nelda, "thank you for seeing me on such short notice."

"Come in and let me see if I can help you." She motioned to a comfortable looking leather chair across from her desk.

They sat across from one another. The doctor leaned back waiting for Nelda to speak, her hand resting under her chin.

"I know Laura had problems in her relationships with family and friends. She must have discussed them with you. It's possible one of them had a strong enough motive to kill her. Could you tell me what she discussed with you?"

"It would certainly be unethical for me to discuss this if she were alive, but under the circumstances I might be of some help. Tell me what you know?"

Nelda was heartened by Long's answer. "Laura and I were at a family reunion in New Orleans the week before she was killed. She told me that Antara was trying to kill her, and might be a bad seed. Meaning, I suppose, that Antara was acting as Laura did at sixteen. You know about how Laura's mother died?"

The doctor opened up a folder on her desk and shuffled through the papers, and picked up a sheet of paper. "Laura and I had many sessions about her loss of memory the night her mother died in the house fire. She was afraid to remember, because she thought she might have started the fire. Her memory didn't come back to her in this office. As for Antara, I suggested that Laura send her to a boarding school. Laura was very close to a nervous breakdown. Neither mother or daughter were good for each other at this point."

"Did she tell Antara that she was going to a boarding school?"

"Yes, but Laura didn't tell me how Antara reacted to this news."

"One more question about Antara. Did Laura ever tell you who Antara's father was?"

"No, she never went near that subject, and even if she had I would not disclose that information."

Nelda squirmed in her chair. She wanted so badly for the doctor to tell all about Laura, but knew it wasn't going to happen. She'd just have to ask the right questions. Nelda continued with the suspects.

"Now, about her brother, Edward," Laura loved him and wanted to have a closer relationship, but the brother only used her as a source to borrow money. He actually thinks she started the fire that killed their mother."

"Yes, I believe her brother did have a certain amount of animosity toward Laura. Since I do not know him, it would be difficult for me to say that his feelings toward her would be a sufficient motive for murder."

"I suppose we're getting down to the end of my list. Laura told me she quit her job, and had broken off her engagement with Thomas Compton, because she didn't like some of the techniques he used in his fertility lab. Did she ever say anything about that?"

"No, and since Mr. Compton is one of my patients. I certainly can't discuss him with you."

Nelda was so disgusted she could cry. Had Thomas become a patient to find out what the doctor knew about his relationship with Laura? The doctor hadn't helped her a bit. Rising from her chair Nelda said, "Thank you doctor for your time."

Long rose too. "I'm sorry. The only other thing I can tell you is that Laura thought someone was spying on her, an old man who was working for her. I've forgotten his name. It could have been her imagination."

"Was it Max Beaux?"

"Yes, does that name mean anything to you?"

Nelda nodded her head. She could still see the cloud of smoke boiling out of his old truck. Blue, it was blue smoke.

CHAPTER TWENTY-THREE

Big Bend Bound

The evening sunshine mingled with mist from Nelda's sprinkler forming a rainbow. Nelda was entranced with its beauty, but time was growing short. Soon the sheriff would be here to pick her up for dinner. How she wished she could just stay home, sit on her back porch and watch the cardinals having an evening meal from the bird feeder under her big oak tree. She had other birds too, but nothing pleased her as much as the beautiful red birds that filled her yard all summer.

With a sigh, she turned off the sprinkler, and had one last glimpse of her crimson friends before heading for the bathroom. Nelda had a habit of locking the bathroom door when she took a bath. It was a habit she'd developed as a child, because she had to share the bathroom with her siblings. When it was her turn, she wanted the bathroom all to herself. After drawing a large tub of water in her old, porcelain lined footed tub, she submerged in a cascade of bubbles. This was the first time she'd completely relaxed in weeks. The mood didn't last long, because someone started jiggling the doorknob. She panicked and looked for a way to defend herself. Struggling out of the tub, she slipped into her cotton robe and picked up a straight back chair. It was then she heard a familiar voice.

"Aunt Nelda, are you in there?"

Nelda put the chair down and opened the door. "Sue, what are you doing scaring me to death?"

"I'm sorry, Aunt Nelda, but you didn't answer when I knocked and rang the back doorbell. I was worried about you and came on in."

"I've got to get that back doorbell fixed. Let me have a hug. I haven't seen you in a week." Nelda embraced Sue and led her to the bedroom.

"Need to start locking your doors too."

"Don't lecture me now. I've got to hurry and get dressed, Joe is taking me to dinner."

"Oh, I see you're on first name terms." Sue raised her eyebrows and smiled.

"Not you too." Nelda groaned as she retrieved fresh lingerie from a large mahogany chest of drawers. "We're just meeting to discuss Laura's case."

"I'm sorry I'm giving you a hard time, Aunt Nelda, I know you're worried about Yvonne Sands. Let's hope she'll show up."

"Alive, I pray," answered Nelda. She slipped into her underwear and guided a soft gray voile dress over her head. "Zip me up, Sue, and tell me why you're paying me a visit."

"Aunt Nelda, you know me too well." She pulled up the zipper and followed Nelda back to the bathroom and perched on a chair. "Mary called and wants you and me to do her a favor."

"What is it?" Nelda asked as she put on her makeup.

"Before Laura died she made some reservations at the lodge in Big Bend National Park. Mary didn't cancel the reservation because Antara begged her not to. It seems our teenager had visions of going hiking in the Chisos Mountains with Derek. But Mary told her the only way she could go was with responsible adults. So guess who Antara chose?"

"You," said Nelda putting the finishing touches on her hair.

"Wrong. Us. The reservations are for next week."

"Impossible, Antara is in school, and I would never trust Derek and Antara together."

Nelda rubbed a little *Dazzling* cologne on her wrists and turned to face Sue.

"Very possible," answered Sue. "Antara is out of school for the summer, Derek has to work, and it just so happens my boss is giving me the week off."

"Your fiancé boss would give you anything. But I have a big problem." Nelda slipped on her white sandals.

"Such as?" Sue asked. She followed Nelda out of the bathroom to a hall closet.

"Who is going to stay in my house and protect it from some nut burning it down?"

"Ha, I got you. Walter will stay in your house while you're gone."

"I suspect a conspiracy," said Nelda removing her handbag from the closet.

"Does that mean you'll go?" Sue clapped her hands together.

"I suppose so, but don't expect me to go on every hiking trail."

"Great! You're a doll. I'll call Antara and make the arrangements. Have fun tonight."

"By the way," asked Nelda, "who was originally supposed to go on that vacation?"

"The reservations were made last year when Laura was still engaged to Thomas. So they were for Laura, Thomas, Antara and Derek."

Sue made her escape quickly as though Nelda might change her mind. Nelda shook her head for being such an old softie. At least she'd now have an opportunity to talk to Antara about her mother's diary.

*   *   *

Joe and Nelda had a corner table at the Vintage Wine Restaurant. There was a lighted candle in the middle of the table and background music with the voice of Johny Mathis singing "Mona Lisa." Nelda was enchanted, because she remembered hearing that same song coming from a juke box in the fifties. How nice it was to be eating out with an attractive man. She hadn't had a date since her husband died. For the next few minutes she lost sight of what her mission for tonight was all about.

The waiter brought a bottle of wine to the table for Joe's approval. It was a 1998 Benchmark Cellars Chardonnay from California. Joe nodded his approval. Why, Nelda thought, does everyone seem to know about good wines but me? This one tasted like vanilla and cinnamon, but with a dry finish.

"What would you like to eat, Nelda? The food here is very good."

Nelda looked at the prices on the menu. "And just what are we celebrating, Joe?"

"Our first meal together." Joe smiled and picked up his glass. "I propose a toast to our friendship and to solving the Finch case."

"I'll certainly drink to that." They brought their glasses together just as the waiter returned to take their order. "I want the Cornish hen stuffed with fruited rice," Nelda said.

"Make that two of those," added Joe.

After the waiter left, Nelda decided it was time to get down to business. "Have you heard any more news of Yvonne Sands?"

"No I haven't. Not a trace of her. She just high-tailed it and left town. Makes me wonder what she was hiding from me when I questioned her."

"I'm afraid she didn't leave Houston, and her body will show up in the ship channel or bay area." Nelda's eyes became moist.

Joe reached across the table and held Nelda's hand. "Don't believe the worst."

"I can't help it. Look at all the things that have happened. Laura was poisoned, my house was set on fire, someone broke into Laura's house, and now Yvonne Sands is missing."

"I'll find out who did those things, but it's going to take time." Joe set his glass down hard.

Withdrawing her hand from Joe's, Nelda looked at him and smiled. "Did I tell you about Sue and me visiting the blind psychic in Louisiana?"

"I can't believe you did that. You just don't seem the type." He shook his head in wonderment.

"It's true. She told me I would have romance, suffering and danger enter my life." Nelda braced herself for his comment.

"Everyone at some point will have those three things occur in their life," said Joe. "Did she say anything else worthwhile?"

"A few other things." She decided not to tell him the fortune teller's warning about the color blue. For some reason, she had very strong feelings about that prediction.

Their conversation came to a halt as the waiter set down a large tray with their entrees. The Cornish hens' aroma was magnificent. She could hardly wait until the two of them were served, so she could begin eating.

"These birds look down right delicious. Let's do this again next week," Joe said.

"I'll be in Big Bend National Park next week, but when I get back it's a date."

"Who are you going with?" Joe looked worried.

"Sue and Antara. Laura made the reservations last year. Walter will be staying in my house while I'm gone"

"That's a long way for three woman to go by themselves."

"You mean without a man. Rest easy, Joe, we won't be taking any chances. We have reservations right in the park, a cabin in the woods."

They ate in silence. Nelda was almost sorry she'd told him about her trip. He worried too much. When they finished eating, he excused himself and returned several minutes later with a package wrapped in brown paper and tied with a string.

"Since you are going on that long trip, this is a good time to give you this as a reminder of me." He handed her the package.

She shook the package. "Can't be chocolates, nothing slides around."

"I doubt that you even eat candy. Open it now." He smiled in anticipation, like a small boy eager to please.

"Well, I won't have to worry about keeping the bow." She untied the string, unfolded the paper and found a box containing a black cell phone.

Nelda was startled; it seemed an odd gift to her. Finally she said, "I guess this is supposed to help me when I'm in trouble?"

"You bet! I've paid for the first month's use, and your number is taped to the side of it." He sat back grinning with his arms folded.

"Okay, you and Sally win. Thank you very much. I'll take this thing with me when I go out." She didn't say she'd turn it on. Nelda was stubborn and saw no reason to change her lifestyle.

Joe paid the bill and they left the restaurant, running through a light drizzle to the truck. Conversation was scarce on the way back to her house. She hadn't shared her visit to Laura's psychologist with Joe, but what was there to share? Long had told him the same thing or had she?

"What did you find out when you visited Laura's psychologist, Joe?" The rain had increased causing Joe to drive slower. He dodged

130

a couple of potholes on Nelda's street, not answering her question until he pulled up in her drive.

"No help at all. Nothing that you and I don't already know, except that Thomas Compton is now the doctor's patient. I find that highly suspicious."

Nelda turned the ring on her finger. "Did Long mention that Laura thought Max was spying on her?"

"No, but I wouldn't be surprised. I know you don't agree with me, but he's my number one suspect."

Not waiting for her reply, Joe got out of the truck and went around to help Nelda step down from the high cab. As they reached her front door, she looked down at the cell phone and wished he had given it to someone else. It was just something more to keep up with, but she appreciated his concern for her.

"Joe, thank you for the phone, good company and wonderful meal. As for Max, he's a basket case, who should have our sympathy. He's still on my suspect list, but so are all the others."

"Take care of yourself, Nelda. I'll be watching the bad guys while you're gone."

After hesitating for just a moment, he put his arms around her and drew her close, then very gently kissed her on the lips. Nelda didn't kiss him back, but she didn't pull away either. The smell of Old Spice engulfed her while she was in his arms. A sense of euphoria remained even after being released. In fact, Nelda felt downright giddy, but fought to gain her composure.

"Next time we'll have dessert here," promised Nelda.

"I think I just had dessert," Joe replied smiling. "But there's one other thing."

"What?" Nelda asked.

"Don't forget to turn your cell phone on when you leave the house."

* * *

"Really, Antara, do you think you're going to need all the junk you have stacked on the driveway?" Sue asked as she helped Nelda load it in the back of her van.

131

Nelda laughed. It reminded her of when she and Sally had gone to Galveston. They didn't use half the stuff they transported to the beach house on the island.

"Okay, I'll leave some here." Antara responded. "But I bet shopping centers are a long way from where we're staying in Big Bend. One bag is filled with survival food and the other with canteens, binoculars and critter books. After all, this is a nature outing."

After Antara made a trip inside, Nelda shouted. "All aboard. We have a long way to go."

"How long?" Antara asked, crawling in the back seat. Sue got in the front.

"Over three hundred miles to Del Rio where we spend the night, and then another two hundred fifty to the lodge. We'll get there tomorrow after lunch."

Nelda backed the station wagon out and they were on their way to the wide open spaces. Her spirits soared and she was happy to leave some of her worries behind. She'd try not to dwell on Laura's death every hour of the day. Putting the case on hold for a while might give her renewed brain energy when she returned. Holding that thought, she started singing and the girls joined her. "It's a long way to Big Bend Country, we've a long way to go." Nelda got a lot of satisfaction watching Antara in her rear view mirror. This raven haired child could not be a killer.

*　*　*

Their overnight stay in Del Rio was uneventful. They were so tired by the time they checked in at the Holiday Inn, all they wanted to do was shower and hit the sack. Nelda didn't have to persuade them to turn the lights out at 11:00 p.m.

After a continental breakfast the next morning, Sue got behind the wheel and they continued on US 90 toward Big Bend Country. They were only a couple of hundred miles from their destination. Antara stretched out on the back seat and went back to sleep, while Nelda opened up the state map. She couldn't see how they could go wrong. It was a straight shot on 90 to Marathon where they would take US

385 into the park Her excitement grew as she read about the trails they might climb in the Chisos Mountains.

"After we check in, Sue, let's take the Chisos Basin Loop Trail. That will be good for starters."

"When was the last time you were here, Aunt Nelda?"

"Several years ago, but we didn't come in the summer time. In this season we need to stay with the mountain climbs. It's going to be hot as Hades in the desert and river valley, but in the Basin where we're going to stay it will be nice, even cool at night. The elevation is 5,400 feet."

They made good highway time, stopping only long enough to eat a sandwich and have a bathroom break. Finally, they were in Marathon, 68 miles from their destination. "If I had known Big Bend was so far away, I wouldn't have come," said Antara. "I'm wondering if the trip is worth it."

"You'll change your mind once we're there," Nelda said, smiling at the tired teenager.

"How big is that park anyway?"

"Oh, it covers 1,252 square miles. There's a lot of wonderful scenery and wildlife to see." Nelda was glad she'd boned up on elevations and area.

They were mostly quiet for the rest of the trip drinking in the terrain that was so different from the Stearn area. Creosote bushes, long stems of lechuguilla and colorful cacti could be seen on either sides of the road. In the distance loomed the mysterious, blue Chisos Mountains where they would do their hiking.

They pulled up at the Chisos Mountains Basin Lodge in early afternoon. Everyone rushed to get outside. Sue looked up at the sky and said, "Get a load of that sky. It looks like a Colorado sky."

What Nelda felt when she looked up made her break out in a sweat. The sky was the purest blue. But why did this disturb her? Nelda looked away and wished she had never visited the psychic. She could sense the eyes of strangers watching them from the lodge windows.

CHAPTER TWENTY-FOUR

Kidnapped

The cabins were located in a secluded area up some distance from the main lodge and restaurant. Their cabin had a small kitchen, living room and two bedrooms. Nelda quickly took advantage of her senior status and moved into the bedroom with the single queen sized bed. No one grumbled, so Nelda knew she'd made the right decision.

All three quickly changed into hiking clothes, which included shorts, T-shirts, and hiking boots. Antara handed out canteens filled with water. She had put initials on the containers with magic marker, so they could tell them apart. Then she strapped on a backpack with trail mix and fruit.

"I suppose we're all set," said Nelda, putting her safari hat and sunglasses on.

They trooped to the trailhead located in the Chisos Basin. "This trail is a little under two miles and climbs 350 ft. We'll have to work into those longer ones."

Walking was not difficult, because there was a gradual climb. Nelda was delighted with the flowers she saw blooming. She even recognized some of them: deep blue tube-flowers, brilliant red paintbrush and pink prickly poppy. All the others could be identified later. Tomorrow she'd have the opportunity to paint those flowers with the watercolors packed in her bag.

The girls walked ahead of Nelda, lifting their binoculars at intervals to watch the birds in flight or gazing at the blue mountain tops that appeared to be just a few yards away. All were enjoying the fresh air and seemingly endless space. Nelda felt guilty for conjuring up some hidden danger here in the park. Was it possible she was trying to make the fortune teller's prophesy come true? It was absurd to think the color blue had foreshadowed all the misfortunes that had occurred. As for strangers watching them, why shouldn't they? Here are two beautiful, young girls traveling with their chaperone.

After finishing the Basin Loop Trail, they made the short Window View Trail just in time to see a fabulous sunset. With darkness on their heels, the threesome hurried back to their cabin for a quick shower before dinner.

In the lobby of the lodge, there was a gift shop. Nelda joined the girls in looking for souvenirs to take home. She bought the official national park handbook, *Big Bend,* and a T-shirt for Sally with colorful cacti splashed all over it. Antara chose a cap for Derek, with a decal of an Aplomado falcon on the bill. Sue chose the book, *Three Steps to the Sky,* for Walter. Satisfied with their purchases they trooped into the dining room. The waitress seated them next to the window that looked out over the desert terrain and took their order. All three ordered vegetables and chicken.

Antara looked somewhat sad before she spoke. "I guess this is my last fling before going to boarding school."

"I heard something about that," said Nelda. "Tell us the details, Antara."

"Before mother died she chose an academy for me to attend my last two years in high school. It's located in Connecticut, a school for young ladies," she said making her voice sound hoity-toity.

Sue and Nelda laughed as Antara lifted her small finger in the air to drink a glass of water.

"I'm glad you decided to give it a try. I know your mother thought it was best," Nelda replied.

"I'll sure miss Derek. Aunt Mary said if I hated it, I could come back home."

Nelda hesitated before she asked the next question, but she just had to know. "Antara, I found a dairy that belonged to your mother hidden in the ceiling over your bed. Did you destroy some pages in it?"

"I did, Nelda, and I knew you would find it when the poster came down. Mother thought either Derek or I had sabotaged her car and it really hurt me. I cut those sheets out of her journal and threw them away. Why would she think such a thing?" Tears formed in her eyes as she twisted on a napkin in her lap.

"I believe deep down she didn't believe that," Nelda reassured her. "She was having some psychological problems, worried about the way she treated her own mother. But thank you for telling me the

135

truth about the journal." Nelda patted Antara on the arm. "We're going to put that behind us now, and have some fun."

All the traveling, fresh air and hiking were getting to Nelda. She was having trouble keeping her eyes open before she finished her meal. "Hey, Guys," she said as they finished eating, "last one back to the cabin has to fix the coffee pot."

"You'll be sorry, Aunt Nelda," laughed Sue as they paid the bill. "You'll wish you were last when you try the coffee tomorrow morning."

Later, as they prepared for bed something troubled Nelda. It was remembering the strangers staring at them when they arrived, but after all, everyone here was a stranger.

Feeling a little foolish, she went into the girls' bedroom and gave an order. "Please put your windows down and lock them."

"Why?" asked Sue. "The cool breeze blowing in feels so good."

"Do it for me, so I can go to sleep." With hands on hips, Nelda tapped out a warning with her foot.

"Okay, worrywart," Sue said grudgingly, "good night."

* * *

Nelda didn't have any trouble locating the Basin Road that took them to Panther Pass. This was the trailhead location for Lost Mine Trail, which climbed 1,100 feet to some fantastic views.

She unloaded her portable easel, stool and watercolors by the side of the road. "Okay girls, as you go up the mountain trail don't forget to sip water from your canteens. The atmosphere is so dry you'll need to replace the fluid you're losing. I'll be waiting for you right here."

"You are so chicken, Aunt Nelda," Sue chided as she shifted her backpack.

"Hey, I said before we started out I wouldn't make all the trails. Somebody has to prove we've really been here by putting it down on art paper."

"Well, paint one for me, Nelda. I especially like the Pricklypear cactus." Antara spoke up as she rubbed sunblock on her body. Her face and arms were red from the previous days' excursion.

136

Nelda waved them up the trail, then busied herself mixing paints. The Claret cup cacti caught her eye as she entered the park. Here was one in full bloom waiting for her to catch the flaming red edges of its petals and yellow insides. Some two hours later, she had an accumulation of cactuses' facsimiles on art paper, including the Pricklypear for Antara. Nelda stretched and adjusted her broad-brimmed hat as she gazed up the trail where the girls had disappeared. She should be hearing from them soon.

As time passed and there was still no sign of her charges, Nelda began to worry. There were mountain lions and certainly black bears in the park, but these creatures were usually scared of humans. All at once she had this terrible urge to do something, anything. Nelda looked through the pocket of her car for the cell phone Joe had given her. She guessed she'd be forced to use it. Just as she started dialing 911, she heard a whoop from Sue. 'Thank God.' Nelda prayed out loud.

Sue stumbled toward her sobbing. "Aunt Nelda, Antara has disappeared!" She stood gasping for breath. "One minute she was ahead of me and then she just vanished. I can't find her anywhere."

"Hold on," said Nelda. "Let's start at the beginning. How far were you up the trail when she disappeared?"

"I don't know, maybe a mile." Sue threw her backpack down and sat on the side of the road.

"Why weren't you'll together?"

"I stopped to look at some of the birds, but Antara didn't want to slow down. I told her to go ahead and I'd soon catch up. After about five minutes, I hurried on up the trail, but never caught sight of her. It's like she vanished."

"Did you hear anything?"

"I could have sworn I heard her laughing, but it must have been my imagination, because she is really gone." Sue started crying again.

"Could she have fallen down the mountain, Sue?"

"It wasn't a difficult climb. I guess she could have, but how could she totally disappear?"

"The closest ranger station is in the basin. I think I've got the number somewhere. In the mean time, we'll just sit tight and see if she shows up." Nelda didn't want Sue to see how really worried she was. She found the ranger station telephone number in a small notebook. After calling the number and explaining what had happened, Nelda paced up and down until the ranger arrived.

If Nelda hasn't been in such a turmoil, she would have enjoyed talking to Mark Berger, the good looking, muscular ranger. His skin was well bronzed from the sun and his muscles stood out from rugged walking in the park. His dark eyes showed concern as Nelda explained why she had called him.

"Now, let me see if I've got this straight," the ranger said. "Your young cousin, Antara, was on the Lost Mine Trail with your niece here and she disappeared?"

"That's right," said Sue rushing up to the ranger. "She was maybe five minutes ahead of me. I had stopped to look at some birds. After that, I rushed to find her, but she was gone, totally disappeared."

"But your aunt said you might have heard her laughing."

"It may have been something else. It must have been, since I couldn't find her," Sue exclaimed.

"Are you too tired to go back up the trail and show me where you were when you stopped to watch birds?"

"No," said Sue picking up her water bottle.

Nelda said, "I'm going too." She opened her car door and threw her art supplies inside, picked up her canteen and locked the car.

The ranger looked at Nelda, "You sure you're up to it?"

"I am and let's hurry. Suppose something has happened to her? I'd never forgive myself."

With the ranger leading the way, they started up the trail. Nelda was bringing up the rear, but she was keeping up with adrenaline flowing.

After an hour or so they came to a grove of junipers. Sue asked the ranger to halt. "This is where I stopped to watch birds in those trees. I know it was here, because I remember sitting on this old log. See how I've brushed off the old bark? Antara couldn't have been more than one-hundred yards ahead of me when I started back on the trail. Then, I really rushed to catch up with her, but never did."

"Okay," said Berger, "let's look carefully on both sides of the trail. There is the possibility she got off the trail and is wandering around out there."

After ten more minutes on the trail, Mark signaled for them to stop. "I see something in those bushes. It looks like a strap of some kind. We have a lot of visitors using this trail and it might be something they discarded."

Nelda held her breath while he investigated. He held up a canteen attached to a strap.

It was just like the ones she and Sue carried. "Are there initials on it?"

The ranger held up the canteen to examine its sides. "There are initials, AF. This may be her canteen. I can't imagine how she could lose it."

Nelda ran up to have a look. She cried out in anguish when she saw the initials. Running ahead of the ranger, she gave full attention to the trail in front of her. It looked as if someone was dragging their feet on the trail.

"Oh my God!" Nelda screamed. "Could some animal be dragging her down the trail?"

The ranger ran to her side. "There are black bears in the mountains and mountain lions too, but most of the time they are afraid of adults. How old is Antara and how big is she?"

"She's sixteen, five six and weighs about one thirty," answered Nelda.

The ranger crouched and studied the ground for clues. "I'm sure animals in the park didn't harm her, especially in the daytime. If anybody was dragging her it would probably be a man. From these signs on the trail, it looks like she's on her own most of the time. Maybe someone is hurrying her along."

"What should we do?" Nelda asked, holding back the tears.

"I'll call the Ranger Station for help. We'll search for her."

"What if someone is forcing her to go with them? Can we catch them before they leave the park?" Nelda bit her lip and waited for the answer she already knew.

"Very little chance. There are several ways to get out of the park and Mexico is in throwing distance, across the Rio Grande."

Nelda and Sue clung to each other. When was this hell going to end, thought Nelda. Here she was responsible for another lost person. For the first time in her life, she felt completely defeated.

CHAPTER TWENTY-FIVE

In Hot Pursuit

Nelda dried her eyes after calling Mary and telling her about Antara's disappearance. Now, she had to let Joe know what was going on. Making the phone call to him would be almost as bad as having to tell Mary. It had to be done. She waited until Sue was out of the cabin, then made the call. When Joe answered the phone, she could tell from his voice he was glad she'd called.

"Nelda, I was hoping to hear from you. How's Big Bend?"

"I'm afraid it's not good news. Yesterday, Antara disappeared," she blurted out.

"What happened?" Joe asked.

"Sue and Antara were climbing a mountain, with Antara up ahead, and all at once she was gone. We found her canteen and from the tracks in the dirt it looked like someone was half dragging her down the trail."

"My God! Did the rangers search for her?"

"Yes. We all tried to find her, but not a trace. They even brought in a dog to look for her but the trail led back to the road. She was either kidnapped or went willingly with whoever it was."

"Did they stop people coming out of the park?"

"They were watching the exits, but there are just too many ways to get out. Maybe she didn't come out at all." Nelda started crying and had to stop talking.

"You're blaming yourself for this, right?"

"I am. I was sitting there painting pictures at the trailhead, while someone probably dragged Antara off. If I'd hiked with the girls, this wouldn't have happened." Nelda gripped the telephone hard.

"Don't take the blame, Nelda. Anyone hell-bent on kidnapping Antara would have gotten to her sooner or later. You know that."

"Have you kept tabs on the suspects at home?" Nelda asked.

"I told you I would, and they did leave town the day after you did."

"Is it possible one of them came here?" Nelda held her breath for the answer.

"Max supposedly went to visit an uncle in Louisiana, borrowed his sister's car. Edward and Thomas are apparently on business trips."

"Where are Edward and Thomas?" Nelda asked. Her hopes were up just a fraction. Was it possible Antara ran off with one of these men? Had Sue really heard Antara laughing?

"Edward is at the Hyatt Regency in the Hill Country, right out of San Antonio, and Thomas has gone to a medical conference in Houston."

"What about Derek, is he on the job?"

"I don't know. I'll check on him. What are you going to do now?"

"Since you've told me about all the suspects leaving town, I feel that she might be with one of them. The only thing to do is find out where those men were yesterday."

"Nelda, come on home and we'll do that."

"Yes, I will, but not right away. I promise to be in touch soon."

After good-byes were said, Nelda knew exactly which suspect she'd check out first. San Antonio was directly in her path going home. The curtain of despair was lifting slightly since she had chosen a course of action.

A weary Sue entered the cabin to find Nelda throwing things into her suitcase. "What's going on, Aunt Nelda? I hope we're not leaving right away, because I am so tired I can hardly keep my eyes open." She pulled off her shoes and threw herself on the bed.

Usually Sue was full of energy, but now everything about her drooped including her beautiful blonde hair. She was the epitome of a worn-out soul. After closing the suitcase quietly, Nelda decided she just had to give Sue a chance to recover before they got on the road again.

"You're right, Sue; we're both tired. How about us sleeping for a couple of hours and then going on to San Antonio? I found out that Edward is there, staying at the Hyatt Regency, right outside the city. I want to see if he's involved with Antara's disappearance."

"I don't know what good it will do to find him. He wouldn't have Antara with him, especially if he kidnapped her." Sue yawned, then turned on her side before continuing in a sleepy voice, "Edward really knows where to hide out..." Her eyes closed and her body became completely motionless. Nelda pulled the sheet over her exhausted niece, and backed out of the bedroom.

*   *   *

The Hyatt Regency Hill Country resort was only twenty minutes from downtown San Antonio. Nelda had no trouble finding the buildings set on two-hundred acres of rolling hills. Sue had visited the resort several months earlier with a group of nurses. She filled Nelda in on what to expect as they entered the lobby.

"This is really a humongous place, Aunt Nelda. It has several hundred guest rooms and over fifty suites."

"Well what is there to do here? Seems to me it would be more fun to be at one of the hotels on the River Walk."

"Lots to do if you have the plastic. There's a golf course, swimming pools, tennis courts, fitness center, walking trails, restaurants and easy access to the Sea World and Fiesta Texas theme parks."

Nelda shook her head as she took in the luxury of the reception area. Couches and chairs, most covered in leather, were arranged in groupings, while Remington-style bronzes of cowboys on horses were displayed upon wooden tables. Beautiful, oil paintings, and other hanging decorations reminiscent of the Old West carried out the resorts western motif.

As Nelda approached the receptionist, Sue pulled her back with a worried look. "You're not going to register here are you? The cost of a room is between two and three hundred dollars."

Her aunt smiled. "Think I'm poor huh? Well I am, but before I spend my money so freely, I'll ask her to call Edward's room, and we'll visit him, then leave."

The young woman behind the counter wore a smart uniform. Her makeup was perfect and every strand of red hair was in place. Was there just a touch of arrogance about her as she looked at the two disheveled travelers before her? Nelda wished she and Sue had taken more time at Big Bend to dress properly instead of wearing shorts and T-shirts.

The receptionist gave them a formal smile as they approached. "And how may I help you?"

"My cousin, Edward Finch, is staying here and I would like to visit him."

"Just one moment please," the girl said as she turned to her computer.

Nelda motioned for Sue to move over and look at the screen. She hoped her niece could take note of Edward's room number. Sue, trying to be as inconspicuous as possible, moved to the other side of the counter, so she could see over the receptionist's shoulder. After calling up Edward's name and room number on the screen, the redhead turned back to Nelda.

"Mr. Finch is registered here. Would you like me to call his room and see if he's available?"

"Yes, I would appreciate that." Nelda kept her fingers crossed, because she didn't know what she would do if Edward wasn't there.

The young woman lifted the phone and dialed. After a few seconds, to Nelda's delight, the receptionist was actually talking to someone in Edward's room. Sue smiled encouragement to Nelda as she leaned wearily on the counter.

Redhead cradled the phone and turned back to Nelda, "Mr. Finch is not in his room."

"Who gave you that information?" Nelda asked.

"A guest in Mr. Finch's room."

Nelda frowned. "May I have the room number? I'll call him later."

"I'm sorry, I can't give out that information."

Of course that was the rule, but Nelda had to ask. She and Sue moved away from the reservation desk and sat on one end of a sofa.

"Who do you suppose is in Edward's room?" Sue asked.

"That's what I want to find out. This is supposed to be a business trip, but I can't imagine a pharmaceutical company being so generous with their employees. Did you read his room number off the screen?"

"Part of it, there were three numbers, 29 something. Sorry I couldn't make out the third number. She kept getting in the way."

"Well what now?" Sue asked.

Nelda chewed on her bottom lip as she studied a brochure about the resort. Finally she spoke. "I see a Sportsman's Bar listed here. If I know Edward, and I think I do, he'll show up there sooner or later."

"Why do you suspect Edward of harming Antara? What has he to gain?"

"Everything, which I understand is considerable. And at the rate he's spending his money, it will be gone shortly."

"Harm his own niece, hard to believe." Sue shook her head sadly.

They walked to the Sportsman's Bar without talking. After they arrived, Nelda made a decision. They would have something to drink, and if Edward didn't come in she would start knocking on second floor doors.

A big screen TV at one end of the lounge was showing an ice hockey game. Nelda shuddered as she watched two players collide. Smaller screens displaying other sports were placed over the bar. They found two empty stools in front of a TV showing a golf tournament with Tiger Woods.

The bartender, a middle-aged man with graying hair, cleaned the bar off in front of them with a white cloth, then draped it over his shoulder. He eyed them pleasantly and asked for their order.

"You want a Coke, Sue?" Nelda asked.

"Sure," she answered, "and how about some veggies to nibble on?"

"Veggies and two Cokes, do you have a designated driver?" The bartender asked, smiling.

"Absolutely," Nelda answered, smiling back. That's what she needed, a bartender with a sense of humor. When he went off to fill their order, she glanced around the room taking note of all the customers present. Edward was not among them.

After they received and paid for their order, Nelda suggested they move to a table near the door. This way they wouldn't be as conspicuous and still be able to see who entered. Sue nibbled on a carrot stick as they made the exchange.

"How long are we going to wait for Edward?" Sue asked. "I'm about ready to head for home."

"Well, I see you've gotten your second wind," Nelda said. "You were so tired a few hours ago, I thought you'd need a blood transfusion to get going."

"I don't know how you do it, Aunt Nelda. You're two and one-half times my age and still going strong."

Nelda smiled. "Someday I'll just crater, but now it's the thought of some slime out there thinking he can get away with murder that keeps me going."

"It would be nice to narrow it down from four suspects to one," answered Sue.

"True," answered Nelda, as she took another sip of Coke. "But now I'm convinced that Antara didn't do it. She's just not capable of causing all the trouble that's happened."

"You mean like the disappearance of her mother's friend, your fire, the break-in, and now her own disappearance?" Sue waited for an answer while munching on a stick of celery.

"Exactly, but it seems we can't pin those criminal activities on the others either. There are so many unanswered questions…"

"Frankly, I think Edward would be an idiot to kidnap and murder Antara just to inherit her money." Sue said. She rubbed the back of her neck and yawned.

Nelda got out of her chair. "We've waited around long enough. Let's go to the second floor and see if we can find Edward's room."

Sue shook her head as she followed Nelda out of the bar. "Please don't tell me we're going to start knocking on doors?"

"Okay, I won't tell you, and I'll do all the knocking."

They walked up the stairs instead of taking the elevator. A young girl, with long black hair braided with beads, was pushing a cart filled with dirty laundry down the hall. Nelda called to her. "Excuse me, Miss, could you tell me where I might find room 290?"

She leaned on the cart before answering. Her round face almost hidden by a pile of towels. "Room 290 is to the right, but it ain't cleaned up yet. You gonna have to wait."

"You don't understand," Nelda said. "I'm not checking in, just looking for my cousin. We know the first two numbers of his room is 29."

"You're out of luck, Lady, 295 is the only one got anybody in it and it shore ain't a man." She snickered.

"Thank you for your help," said Nelda as she turned to the right with Sue several steps ahead of her.

The maid gave them an indifferent look while she continued pushing the cart toward the service elevator. Some of the colored beads in her hair looked as if they might be florescent. Nelda hoped she wouldn't be around long enough to see the maid's head glow.

Sue stopped in front of 295 while Nelda hurried to caught up with her. "Okay, Sue, I'm going to knock."

"I never doubted it," answered Sue.

After tapping lightly on the door, Nelda took a step backwards. She didn't know what to expect when the occupant came to the door. Several seconds later the door opened, and to Nelda's surprise Edward stood there barefooted, with glistening wet hair. His white silk robe was drawn tightly around his body. She had never noticed it before, but he looked a lot like Bert Reynolds, had almost as much acting talent, too. However, the look on his face now was no act. He was shocked at their appearance at his door.

"Nelda," he said with a forced smile, looking from her face to Sue's. "What are you two doing here? I thought you were in Big Bend."

"I'm sorry to impose. Has the sheriff called you yet?"

"The sheriff? Well as a matter of fact he did leave a message for me to call him, but I've been out. What's going on?"

"Someone kidnapped Antara while she was hiking." Nelda couldn't tell by his face if this news was new to him or not.

"No! You mean she's still gone?" He sagged against the door.

"Yes." Nelda heard someone running water in the bathroom. She just had to know who that was. "Do you mind if we come in and tell you about it?"

"It's not a good time for company, Nelda. Could I meet you for breakfast?"

147

"We're driving through. Just thought you might be interested in your niece's welfare." Nelda was so dismayed. She knew her chances of finding out who was in the room with Edward were gone.

Before he could respond, a beautiful girl with auburn hair and green eyes pushed him aside and gave them a dazzling smile. Edward opened his mouth, but no words came out.

"I'm Angelique," she said, holding her short, black robe together with one hand.

Nelda knew then that Edward had been far too busy to kidnap anyone.

CHAPTER TWENTY-SIX

A Voice in the Dark

The sight of Nelda's ancestral home usually filled her with a warm feeling, but not on her return to Stearn from Big Bend National Park. She didn't know what was happening to her; her nervous system was in overload. The weird case was getting out of hand. Sally needed to be here so she could hash things out.

After methodically unpacking her bag, Nelda carried her dirty clothes to the utility room. She then checked her messages. Most of them were from solicitors, but Sally had left a message too. Eagerly, she pressed the play button. "Nelda, Mary has called me about Antara. I'm coming to see you today. Be there in the morning. I'll have to bring Sugar, but you know he's no problem."

Laughing and crying, Nelda sought refuge in the kitchen. How did that old cliché go? *Be careful what you wish for.* On top of all her other problems, Sally was bringing that old, brown dog, Sugar, to spread hair throughout the house. Oh well, what else could happen. She'd put the coffee pot on, and things were bound to get better. As the coffee dripped, Nelda heard the telephone ring. Reluctantly, she picked it up on the fourth ring. It was Joe.

"Hello, Nelda, glad you're home."

"I have mixed feelings about that, Joe. It seems to me I should be back in Big Bend looking for Antara." Nelda picked up the coffee pot and poured coffee into a mug while listening to the sheriff's response.

"You can be assured Antara is long gone from there. Let's thrash it out over dinner tonight."

"We have a complication. My good friend, Sally, is coming to visit and should be here any minute." Nelda stirred sugar and cream in her coffee and took a long sip.

"No problem, I'll take you both."

She couldn't pass up the opportunity to find out if Joe knew something she didn't know. "That's generous of you. We'll be ready at seven," she said before hanging up.

Finishing her coffee, Nelda went back to the problem she'd soon be facing, Sugar. What in the world did I do with that old dog's bed? Nelda wondered. What an aggravation Sugar will be. Sally is positively silly over that mutt. She headed for the hall closet to store her suitcase. Just maybe the dog bed was also stored in there. When she opened the closet door, out tumbled some of the boxed foods Antara had left behind when they went to Big Bend. Nelda sat in the hallway and sobbed about her failure to keep her young cousin safe. She had to find out where Antara was. How could she entertain Sally with so much on her mind? Nelda sought comfort in a tub of hot water.

After a long soak in the bathtub, Nelda's nerves were under control. Thawing out food to feed her guest lunch would be her next project. There was absolutely nothing fresh in the frig. After dressing, she pulled a chicken and wild rice casserole out of the freezer, hoping it would go well with whatever canned vegetable she could find. Fortunately, there were still a few cans of vegetables in the pantry. She was all set for the noon meal. Joe would take care of them tonight.

There was someone pounding on the back door. Nelda hurried to answer. She'd forgotten to have the back doorbell fixed before she left. When she opened the door, an explosion of brown fur jet-propelled into the room knocking her out of the way. It was Sugar's way of saying hello.

Sally stood in the doorway smiling, with just a hint of worry in her blue eyes. "Nelda, I'm happy you're back home. I've been worried to death about you ever since Mary called."

"Come on in. Sugar sure was glad to see me."

Moving slowly, Sally limped across the room trying not to put very much weight on her left foot. Her ankle was tightly wrapped in an elastic bandage.

"What's wrong with your ankle, Sally?" Nelda asked. She looked around for Sugar, hoping the dog had settled down. She didn't see him anywhere.

"I was walking with Sugar. We met another dog and he got pretty excited, wrapped his leash around my ankle. It's almost well now."

Nelda shook her head. She could see that Sally and Sugar were going to be a tremendous help in solving the case.

Nelda hugged Sally's neck. "You should have stayed home with that sore ankle. Come on back to the kitchen. I think Sugar was headed that way."

"Where else would a hungry dog go?" Sally answered.

Sure enough, Sugar was searching for crumbs on Nelda's kitchen floor. When he didn't find any, he sat down at Nelda's feet and looked up at her.

"What a beggar," said Nelda, laughing. "How about me giving him a dog bone in the backyard, Sally? He can't get out. Maybe then we can visit."

"Sure, he probably needs to water some of your bushes anyway."

Nelda had dog bones from the last time Sugar visited. She got one out of the pantry and opened the back door for Sugar. He didn't need any encouragement.

Nelda turned back to Sally. "I'll get you some coffee, then we'll sit in some comfortable chairs on the back porch, so we can watch Sugar and visit at the same time."

A few minutes later, they were sitting in Nelda's rocking chairs on the porch watching Sugar chase a bright yellow, Sulfur butterfly. He'd already caused the dog bone to vanish.

"You know, Sally, ever since Laura died my life has been a nightmare. This last episode with Antara is almost too much to bear. It's as if I'm helping the killer to accomplish his warped goal. I just wonder if Antara would still be with us if I had refused to go to Big Bend."

"Of course not. The killer would have found a way to kidnap her. But why, Nelda?" Who benefits from Antara being out of the picture?"

"Three people possibly: Edward, if she's found dead, would get all his parents' money and Max would get satisfaction, because of his weird need for revenge."

"You said three. What about Laura's ex fiancé? Is there any reason he's want to do Antara harm?"

"I've been giving that a lot of thought. Now suppose Thomas was doing something illegal in his lab, and Laura knew it. Wouldn't he want to do away with the friends and family that Laura confided in?"

"I guess, but what illegal things can one do in a fertility clinic?" Sally asked.

Sugar dashed up on the porch knocking over a watering can. Nelda got up to fill the can with water. She poured water in an empty flower pot saucer for the rambunctious canine before answering.

"There's been a lot of research in stem cell development and also in cloning. From what I can understand, those techniques can include illegal areas. I know the legality part is not going to stop some scientists. Could Thomas be one of those scientists, experimenting in an area that's taboo?" Nelda asked the question more to herself than Sally.

"He's been working with human egg cells and sperm long enough to know what can be done with them." Sally commented.

"Yes, he told me he's been at it for twenty years." Nelda wandered over to a fern hanging basket and started breaking off dead fronds.

"So, you haven't ruled anybody out?" Sally reached down to give Sugar a pat. He jumped off the porch and trotted over to an oak tree where a big gray squirrel was descending.

"Oh, but I have. I've ruled out Antara and probably Edward." Nelda smiled and turned toward Sally.

She told Sally all about the visit to Edward's room. Sally especially enjoyed the description of Edward's face when Angelique introduced herself to them.

"Well, why is he still on your list if you think he was too busy to kidnap Antara?"

"There is a chance he hired someone to do the dirty work."

A great commotion caused them to break off their conversation. Sugar barked loudly as a squirrel flicked his tail and stood his ground. Finally, Sugar tired of the game; he returned to the porch as the squirrel scurried away to the next yard.

"You can tell he's getting old," said Sally. A few years ago, he would have been there till doomsday if the squirrel hadn't retreated.

"I hear my phone ringing. You and Sugar come back in and lock the door."

Answering the phone on the fifth ring, Nelda was surprised to hear Joe's voice again.

"Nelda, sorry to have to break our date tonight, but I'm needed. Seems there is some horse rustling going on in the next county, and they asked me to help guard some pastures tonight. Can't turn 'em down, they've helped me too many times."

"I'm disappointed, Joe, but I understand. Let's get together tomorrow. I really need to talk to you."

"We'll definitely go out for dinner tomorrow night. In the meantime, I've got a report for you. Max Beaux, Edward Finch and Thomas Compton are all back in the area. Don't do anything foolish, and take that cell phone with you if you go out."

Nelda did a fast burn. "Sure thing!" She banged the telephone down hard.

"What's wrong, Nelda? You having a lover's spat?" Sally grinned at her friend.

"Oh please, Sally, don't start. I've been doing quite well for a number of years without that chauvinist wonder, but he doesn't seem to realize that."

"I'm sorry, Nelda, Joe must be from the old school, and he'll probably never change. So, if you like him, accept him the way he is."

"You're right, but I'm not going to wrestle with that problem now. He's working tonight, so I guess you're stuck with my cooking."

"Suits me, I came because I thought you needed me, not to be entertained."

Nelda's heart melted. Could there ever be a better friend? She didn't think so.

* * *

Dinner was over and the dishes were in the dishwasher. Nelda and Sally sat side by side looking at the album containing pictures of Laura's growing up years. Nelda had forgotten to give the book to Mary. Hopefully, someday it would be a keepsake for Antara. One picture had been made on Laura's sixteenth birthday. The white lace dress she wore accentuated the loose, black curls that hung down in straight lines. They resembled coiled springs.

"If they had given Laura an electric shock that caused her hair to stand out, stretched a tee shirt over her breast, and pulled tight jeans over her bottom, you'd have Antara," said Nelda.

Sally spoke up. "It's uncanny isn't it? I've never seen a mother and daughter look more alike." She closed her eyes and massaged her ankle as she spoke.

"Okay, I know it's early, but it's off to bed for you. You need to get off that ankle. Watch some TV in the bedroom. We'll talk tomorrow."

Just as Nelda made sure Sally had everything she needed, the phone rang again. "Must be Sue, too late for someone trying to sell me something," she muttered reaching for the phone.

It was Dennis. He said, "It's about the old Finch place. Max saw someone hanging around there this afternoon. He thought you'd like to know about it."

"What was Max doing out that way?"

"We take care of a place near there. Max was out mowing."

"Well, Dennis, it's nice of you to report that, but why not to the sheriff?"

"Nelda, you know how I feel about that guy. He's bad news. Won't give ex-cons a chance to go straight. Look at the way he's treated Max. I tried to call Mary Finch, but nobody answers. Probably nothing to it, but I know there's furniture still in the house."

"Thanks, Dennis, I'll see if I can get someone to go out and check the place."

Nelda knew Joe was out of pocket, but she could call his deputy. Then she remembered how Deputy Carl Hank always seemed to make matters worse. That's when she decided to do her own checking at the old Finch place.

Before leaving, Nelda peeped in the guest bedroom. She found Sally fast asleep with Sugar settled in at the foot of her bed. Nelda decided to leave a note in the kitchen in case Sally woke up and started looking for her. That done, she picked up her keys, and at the last minute stuffed the cell phone in her purse.

The seven o'clock news was just coming on the car radio as Nelda made her way out to the country. It was not dark yet, but Nelda turned on her lights. Twilight was a dangerous time to drive, especially with all the students from the nearby college back in school. As she rolled down Black Prairie Road, she wondered if she had made the right decision. What if she did find some intruders in the house. What then? She supposed she'd be forced to call the deputy. Maybe he had improved as Joe said he had, but Nelda had her doubts.

Oakwood Estates loomed ahead. As she turned into the entrance, a feeling of loneliness engulfed her. She couldn't see the homes from the road, because they were hidden behind screens of thick woods and underbrush. Finally, she arrived at Laura's mailbox. Nelda cut her lights off and drove up the driveway very slowly. She could see the glow from the outside lights. They had light sensors and automatically came on at dusk. There was no movement about the place that she could detect as she came to a halt. Grabbing her car keys, Nelda placed her small, cell phone in the pocket of her pants. She quietly emerged, and headed for the front door.

It was eerie making her way across the porch with so little light. The hanging baskets appeared as giant spiders waiting to pounce on her. She tried opening the front door with a key that she still had, but the dead bolt was in place. Reluctantly, Nelda turned and walked down the drive to the back door. Trees and bushes grew close to this entrance making it difficult to see if anyone was lurking there. After some consideration, Nelda got back in her car and turned on the lights. There was no point in taking any more chances.

A rustling sound in the backseat of the car heightened Nelda's awareness of the odor that permeated the inside, the smell of sweat and gasoline. Someone was back of her breathing heavily, drowning out the pounding of Nelda's heart.

"I knew you'd come, Nelda Simmons, I knew you'd come," whispered the gruff voice from the back seat. A harsh laugh escaped from his throat.

Fear grabbed her and she froze. Before she could react and respond to the voice, she felt a deadening pain in her head. The world went black.

CHAPTER TWENTY- SEVEN

The Ties That Bind

Opening her eyes, Nelda realized she was on the carpet in Antara's old bedroom in the log house. A ray of light from the adjoining bathroom allowed her to see the objects in the room. She wanted to reach up and rub her aching head, but found her wrists securely bound in front of her with that clear plastic tape used to seal boxes. Her whole body ached, especially her legs. When she tried to straighten them, she found her ankles were also bound together with the same kind of tape. Nelda knew from experience this plastic material was extremely difficult to tear or break. If she only had a knife!

A soft moan startled Nelda; it came from the bed. Closing her eyes, Nelda offered up a prayer of thanksgiving to God. She believed that moan came from Antara. As Nelda moved to a sitting position, pain radiated from the spot on her head where she'd received the blow. The move made her quite woozy, but she was determined to see if it really was her young cousin in bed.

Peeking over the mattress, she sighed in relief. Indeed it was Antara, but not bound in tape. She didn't need to be, because she was unconscious; probably drugged, thought Nelda.

"Antara, sweetheart, can you hear me?" There was silence; no more moans escaped from the young girl's lips.

Nelda had monumental tasks facing her. Somehow she had to free herself from the tape, and get Antara to safety before the kidnapper returned. She remembered seeing razor blades in the medicine cabinet over the lavatory when she stayed in this bedroom.

Could she make it to the bathroom? Nelda stood and tried hopping, but that didn't work. Her ankles were bound so tightly, she was afraid she'd lose her balance and fall, and with no free hands available to break the fall, she'd surely fracture something. Okay, scooting would be the only way to go. And scoot she did, suppressing the urge to scream out at every painful motion.

It seemed that it took her forever to reach the bathroom. She could see her watch plainly now; it was 1:30 a.m. Nelda remembered waking up several times after the blow to her head, but promptly went back to sleep. What a stupid mistake she had made coming here all alone. Joe wouldn't be proud of her performance so far. It was then she felt for her cell phone. Gone! It was gone, the one time she desperately needed it.

Slowly, Nelda pulled herself up to a standing position by grasping the commode seat. She opened the medicine cabinet and gave a little gasp. Someone had cleaned it out.

Using both hands, she searched every shelf as best she could. On the top shelf in the very corner she located an old blade stuck in between the shelf and the back of the cabinet. After a few minutes of working it with her fingers and incurring several nicks, it finally came loose. Clutching it in one bloody hand, she sat on top of the john and cried.

Wiping her eyes and nose on the sleeve of her blouse, Nelda went to work. She first used the blade to cut through the tape on her ankles. It worked well and in no time her ankles were free. Nelda massaged her swollen ankles with her sore fingers for a minute to encourage circulation.

Thank goodness her wrists were taped in front of her instead of behind. Regardless, freeing them would take some doing, because they were bound crossed, and Nelda's fingers couldn't reach the tape. The only thing to do was wedge the razor blade in some sort of vise.

When she limped back into the bedroom, she repressed the urge to check on Antara. Each second was precious now; the kidnapper was sure to return at any time.

Nelda tried several different ways to secure one edge of the razor blade, but none worked. Finally, she solved the problem by sitting on the floor and placing the razor blade against the side of the vanity. She held the blade in place with her foot, leaving one sharp edge sticking out vertically. It was going to be a challenge not to injure her wrists as she penetrated the layers of plastic. Carefully, Nelda cut through a layer of the tape. After biting and gnawing the first layer, she succeeded in pulling it away from her wrists. She was sorry to abuse her front teeth in this arduous task, but even without dental insurance it didn't slow her down. She ripped the layers one by one.

"Hallelujah," Nelda exclaimed softly after pulling the last layer of tape from her wrists. Her celebration was cut short by the bedroom door opening with a bang. Thomas Compton stood in the shadowy light. He held a gun in one hand and two blue file boxes in the other. Nelda recognized the files from her visit to the fertility clinic.

Thomas looked at Nelda with eyes wide and raised eyebrows. "What in the hell are you doing here, Nelda?" He set the files down on the vanity.

This wasn't the person Nelda expected. Her mouth flew open in astonishment. "You don't know! Did you send someone to bash my head in, truss me up in tape like an animal, then drag me up here?"

"What a fantastic imagination, I wouldn't do that to you, Nelda. All I've ever wanted from you was for you to butt out of my business. That's why I tried to get you to focus on someone else by burning your kitchen, and going all the way to Big Bend to kidnap Antara. But no, somehow you followed me here."

Nelda worried about Antara. She sat on the bed, put her thumb on Antara's wrist and felt her pulse. It was slow, but strong. She was still completely out.

"What have you done to this child?"

"Antara is just fine, Nelda. In a couple of hours she'll be back to her old self."

Thomas pulled the vanity bench out and sat down. He still held the gun on her, and was entirely too calm to suit Nelda.

"Explain to me what this is all about, Thomas." You can start with Laura's death. I witnessed the toast exchanged between the two of you. You dissolved some of the strychnine in whiskey, didn't you, and mixed it in her lemonade?"

"You're clever, Nelda. How could I ever dissolve those crystals, if I didn't use alcohol? Laura and I toasted each other many, many times during the last few years. It was only fitting for us to have one last toast."

Nelda couldn't believe what she was seeing. A tear ran down Thomas's cheek. He was actually crying, this murderer, this child abductor.

"Did you also tamper with her brakes?"

"I confess, I did. It didn't get the job done."

"Tell me why you killed her. I've got to know."

"I owe you that much, Nelda, because you'll never leave this house alive."

Nelda shrank back against the wooden headboard, pulled a pillow over her chest, and waited for him to continue.

"All my life I've wanted to be a success and have money to prove it. My father said I didn't have guts enough to succeed. Everything I ever did he condemned; nothing I did was good enough. I set out to prove him wrong and I have, but it's too late. The bastard is dead. The proof is in these files," he said, touching them with reverence. I'm going to be rich and I'm going to be famous."

"What does any of that have to do with the murder of Laura? How did she stand in your way?"

"Laura didn't approve of me cloning body parts. That's what my second lab was all about. She thought it was wrong and didn't want any part of it. How could I trust her not to blow the whistle on me? This country is not ready for me either. I'm clearing out, Nelda. Going to a country that appreciates me."

"If you loved Laura, you wouldn't be taking her daughter with you. I suppose that's what you intend to do. Why Antara? She's still a child."

"You don't get it do you? Haven't you wondered why Antara is so much like her mother?"

"What are you saying, Thomas?"

"Antara was cloned from Laura. My very first success." Thomas smiled at Nelda's open mouth. "I was the one that searched Lara's room to find out if she'd taken any proof of the cloning. She didn't."

"I don't believe it," Nelda said emphatically, "and I pray you haven't spoken about this in front of Antara." Nelda glanced over at the still body of the teenager.

"She doesn't know, and I'm not going to spook her. Antara will learn to love me as Laura loved me." His eyes caressed the sleeping body.

"Monster!—that's what you are."

"Time is short, Nelda, perhaps we'd better go downstairs and get this over with. I don't want Antara to see you dead. As soon as she's able to walk we're clearing out forever."

A whiff of acrid air suddenly filled Nelda's nostrils. She looked past Thomas and saw a column of blue smoke in the hallway. *Nelda sees blue.* My God, she had suspected it was Max who attacked her, and now he must have set the house on fire. His revenge this time included whoever was in the house.

Thomas jumped up as the smoke poured into the room. He grabbed his files and stuck them under one arm, and headed for the bed where the drugged Antara lay. "Nelda, you've got to help me get Antara downstairs. Together we can save her."

"Put that gun away before you accidentally kill her. She's dead weight now and you're going to have to use both hands to save her. I'll help all I can."

"These files go with me; you'll have to be my other hand." He placed the gun in his pocket and pulled the sleeping girl to a sitting position. She would have to be carried downstairs. Nelda placed one of Antara's arms around her neck and helped pull her to a standing position. Thomas would have to furnish most of the strength, because Nelda's whole body ached. With their arms around her waist and her arms around their necks, they slowly dragged her to the stairs. The smoke was thickening, but Nelda couldn't see any flames. Adrenaline kept Nelda moving down the stairs. Her head throbbed with every step.

The kitchen was on fire. Flames leaped through the door into the living room following a trail of some kind. Nelda felt sure it was a petroleum product poured by Max while she and Thomas talked upstairs. Thomas looked toward the flames and stumbled. Papers and diskettes from his blue files fell out and covered the stairs. He let go of Antara and started scrambling to pick up his precious research material. Nelda seized this opportunity to continue pulling Antara toward the front door. The fire raced on, heading for the stairs. The killer didn't look up, he continued with his desperate attempt to save the contents of his files.

Nelda didn't know where the strength came from, but she pulled Antara outside and into the driveway. The sleeping girl was awakening, making whimpering noises. Nelda stroked her back to comfort her.

Looking back toward the house, Nelda smelled the burning pine logs as the whole house was engulfed in bright red and yellow flames. The logs sizzled and popped in the giant bonfire. Thomas never had a chance to escape with the files that held his dreams. Nelda was filled with sadness caused by painful memories from the past. She saw the ghostly shapes of all the dead relatives who had lived in this home float upward toward the sky as smoke, *blue smoke.*

*   *   *

Nelda knew Max was out there watching his wonderful display of fire power. He would have been drawn to it as surely as a moth is drawn to the luminance of a light bulb. But later he'd try to find them. Where was superman when she needed him the most?

Hidden in the shrubbery by the driveway, Nelda watched the road, praying for someone to rescue them. She whispered to the weak and groggy Antara not to make a sound. Nelda feared Max as much as she had Thomas. The old guy was nuttier than Sally's Christmas fruitcakes.

And what about help from Sally? Nelda knew she'd found the note by now. Surely Sally had called somebody and told them she hadn't come home. But what if she didn't see the note, or look in Nelda's bedroom? The battle was not over. Another killer waited silently in the woods.

Now that it was growing light, Nelda could see her Ford had escaped damage from the fire. It was covered with ashes but otherwise seemed unharmed. Thank goodness there was no wind and she had parked a good distance from the house. "Antara, do you think you could make it to my station wagon?"

"Maybe with your help, Nelda. I'm still feeling weak."

"It's only fifty feet away. We have to move fast, because I think Max is still hanging around."

The girl shivered. Nelda picked up a tree limb in one hand and held on to Antara with the other. If everything went right, she'd find her extra car key secured to a magnet under the left front fender.

Slowly they made their way to the car. Once there, Nelda opened the door for Antara and helped her get in. She then went over to the other side and groped under the car for the key. Thank God! She had it. Almost there, don't waste time, she thought. As she got in the driver's seat and slammed the door, Max came roaring out of the woods. His face was contorted with hate. Quickly, she locked the doors as he swung a garden rake into the windshield. It bounced off, but Nelda wasn't waiting for the next blow. She started the car and accelerated as Max attempted another attack on the car. He fell to the ground as she sped away.

After traveling a mile, Nelda guided her station wagon to the side of the road and stopped. She pulled Antara close to her and they both burst into tears. "The nightmare is over, baby, the nightmare is over. You're safe now."

Joe found them that way a few minutes later. He pulled Nelda gently out of the car. "Oh Nelda," Joe said holding her tightly. "Sally found your note about five and called. I never expected to find you alive."

"You almost didn't," answered Nelda, "but I've got a story to tell."

* * *

Nelda felt compelled to invite friends and relatives involved in the case so they could find out the facts concerning Laura's death. Joe stood by the mantel waiting to help her with answers. Sally and Mary occupied the sofa; Antara and Derek, holding hands, made themselves comfortable on the carpet; Sue and Walter sat in dining room chairs; Dennis slumped in a rocking chair with his eyes downcast, looking sad. Edward didn't bother to acknowledge Nelda's invitation. He was somewhere in the Bahamas.

"I want to welcome all of you tonight," Nelda said. "I know that we can't bring Laura back, but at least we have the satisfaction of knowing who was behind her death. And we sure want to celebrate Antara's return. It's been a horrible, heart-breaking experience for us, but it's over, thank God. I'll let Joe tell you about Max and his part in this tragedy.

Joe drummed his fingers on the mantle. He looked over at Dennis before he spoke. "Society did a number on Max, condemning his daddy's property. His revenge was to set fires and even when he was caught they couldn't rehabilitate him. This last fire killed Thomas and almost cooked Nelda and Antara. He's back in the prison hospital now, and at his age will probably never get out."

Looking over at the dejected Dennis, Nelda stood. "You shouldn't feel bad for wanting to help Max, Dennis. You had no way of knowing he still had problems."

"I almost got you and Antara killed, Nelda," said Dennis with tears in his eyes.

"No, you didn't. You were only helping an old man by hiring him."

"Sheriff," asked Antara, "did he confess to setting the first fire in our house that killed my grandmother?"

"He did. You mother didn't set that fire." Max didn't admit to it before, because he didn't want to be charged with your grandmother's death."

Antara smiled through her tears. "Mother can rest easy now. She always thought she might have done it." Derek pulled Antara close.

"Nelda, what about Thomas?" Mary asked. "What was all this business about him cloning body parts and why, for goodness sake, did he kidnap Antara?"

Nelda knew she'd have to be careful with her answer. "Well, he claimed he was successful at cloning body parts, but Laura thought it was unethical and was going to tell on him. That's the reason he killed her. As for Antara, he loved her for being Laura's daughter."

"He was a nut case, too" Derek blurted out.

"Perhaps," answered Nelda. "Walter and his committee of physicians couldn't find any record of cloning in Thomas's second lab, and the Chinese assistant has vanished. We don't know what was in the files that burned with Thomas."

"We've got one person unaccounted for," Sue said. "Has Yvonne's body been found?"

"Oh yes," said Joe with a big smile. "We found Yvonne several weeks ago, and we've been keeping her under wraps."

"How horrible," scolded Mary. "Why have you kept this from us, Joe?"

Yvonne came dancing in from the kitchen. She looked as lovely as ever. "Here I am, and thanks to your sheriff for saving my life. After I received a death threat over the phone, Joe insisted I hide out until the murderer was caught. That's what I did."

"Did you know Thomas was the murderer?" Sue asked.

"Not a clue," answered Yvonne. "Laura shared lots of things with me, but her relationship with Thomas and his work was taboo. She didn't discuss it, but he didn't know that."

"What about you, Nelda, when did you realize Thomas was guilty?" Walter asked.

"I really wasn't sure until he walked in with a gun. I thought it was Max who had bashed my head in, because whoever it was smelled like an unwashed laborer. Thomas had a fetish for cleanliness. But the two bad guys overlapped in their meanness. Max discovered Antara drugged in the house, so he lured me out there by telling Dennis someone was lurking around Laura's home. I'm sure he intended to torch the house, but having Antara and me in it added extra fuel to his fire."

"I think you always leaned toward Thomas as the bad guy, Nelda," Joe said.

"It's true, I didn't know why he wanted to kill Laura. However, as a scientist, he would know that strychnine crystals dissolve in alcohol, and I saw him encouraging Laura to make that toast at the birthday party."

"The ending to this mystery is not all bad, Aunt Nelda," said Sue. We can celebrate you, Antara and Yvonne being safe."

"Nelda didn't feel like celebrating, but Sue had insisted on bringing champagne and cake." She and Sue hurried to the kitchen followed by Sally, hobbling along on her bad ankle. Sugar escaped from the kitchen and ran in to join the party.

Bubbles danced in the glasses as they were passed out to everyone including the two teenagers, this being a special occasion. "Joe you make the toast," Nelda said.

"A special toast to the man upstairs, and the health and happiness of new friends." Joe smiled as his eyes met Nelda's.

After their toast, Sally suggested Yvonne sing something cheerful. Yvonne set her glass down and belted out an oldie, "Blue Skies."

Sue and Nelda exchanged looks and burst out laughing. Nelda felt the bad, blue omen was over, done with and kaput, if there ever was one. She joined the others in singing, "nothing but blue skies from now on," while Sugar howled in unison.

CHAPTER TWENTY-EIGHT

Finding Jimmy Nigh

Winter had arrived in Stearn, Texas. Ice glistened on the grass and needles of the big pine tree in her front yard. Nelda and Sally were seated on the velvety, green sofa drinking their morning coffee, and soaking up heat from a cozy fire in the brick fireplace.

Nelda's face was thoughtful and sad. Laura's childhood photograph album was in her lap. "Sally, I've been thinking about this for some time. Did I ever tell you that Laura whispered something to me before she died?"

"I think you did mention a name that made no sense. Have you figured out what she was trying to say?"

After taking a sip of coffee, Nelda responded. "At that time I thought she said, 'Take care of Jimmy Nigh.' But after reflecting on what Thomas told me, I think she was saying Gemini, which means twin."

"Why would she say a thing like that? She must have been out of it."

Nelda picked the album up and held it in her arms. "I've never told a soul about this, but I've got to tell you."

Sally sat up straight and slipped her glasses back in place. Confidences between old friends were not to be taken lightly. "It must be very serious, Nelda."

"It is. Thomas confided in me that Antara was cloned from Laura."

Sally opened her mouth and gasped. "Surely you don't believe that? The man was crazy. We all know the first mammal cloned was that sheep, Dolly, just a few years ago."

"I really don't know what to think. We don't know how long some nations have worked with cloning. Thomas's assistant was from China."

Sally shook her head. "With the population China has, I'm sure they need clones."

NELDA SEES BLUE
A Murder Mystery

"Some people never want to die, Sally. Maybe that's how they expect to live forever. Anyway, suppose it's true. Laura could have asked me to take care of her idential twin, by saying the word Gemini. And then I started thinking about Antara's name."

"She's named after a star, isn't she? There's a star named Antares."

"I know that," answered Nelda, "but that's not the way Antara spells her name." She got up and walked to the bookcase and took out a big dictionary. "You're the English teacher. What word could you substitute for a twin?"

"Let's see. There's *identical, similar...*"

"*Other*, Sally, *other*, the remaining one." Nelda put the dictionary down and started pacing the floor.

"And what did you find when you looked up other?" Sally got up and grabbed the dictionary.

"In that old collegiate dictionary you'll find that `other' comes from the word `antara' in the ancient Indo=Aryan language, Sanskirt."

"For Heaven's sake, Nelda! You've pieced it all together, and I think you halfway believe that Antara is a clone."

"I don't know what to think, but I've decided that no one will ever be able to find out." She opened the album and took out the packet containing Laura's hair. "This is the only part of Laura that wasn't cremated. If someone wanted to, they could prove or disprove Thomas's statement with a strand of her hair. They'll never have that chance." She threw the packet in the fire.

Sally and Nelda clinked their cups together as the fire consumed the evidence.

Both women sat back down and Nelda suddenly smiled at Sally. "We badly need a vacation, Sally. What do you think of a nice cruise on a fun ship?"

"Suits me. You wont be visiting any fortune tellers before we leave will you?"

Both doubled over with laughter. Nelda felt so good she decided to call Joe and invite him over for chicken gumbo.

167

Helen Sheffield

ABOUT THE AUTHOR

Helen F. Sheffield is the author of one previous Nelda mystery, *Nelda Sees Red.* She is also the creator of many mystery stories. Helen and her husband have retired to a retreat outside College Station, Texas where they write full time surrounded by woods and wildlife. Nelda's next adventure will be *Nelda Sees Green.*

Printed in the United States
754100007B